KARMIC LOVE

A novel by
SIR PATRICK BIJOU

CONTENTS

CHAPTER ONE

Blake: Growing

The wind had picked up speed and an arctic rain was pelting down on my thin leather jacket like a multi-tailed whip. As I bent over the icy metal rail on top of the concrete parapet that came up to my waist; the frothy brown water seemed to beckon more and more. With all the seasonal rain typical for the end of January in this part of Germany, the river had probably dug to at least twenty-five feet deep and ten-foot-deep of the torrent, murky water – perfect for swallowing up the disgusting waste of space I had become.

Only a year ago I'd been on top of the world. Granted, an almost 400 lbs. the guy being on top of anything inevitably led to indents, cracks or breaks, but at 6'4" I carried it pretty well. Plus, a lot of it was muscle and the skinnier guys at the garage were happy to let me do the heavy lifting. And there *was* a lot to that, to be the one. It seemed with every year more orders were pouring in: checkups, tuning, tire changes, the works, and our small team of four rapidly accumulated over time. Good mechanics were hard to come by in general, a fact made even worse by the younger generation being increasingly unwilling to put down their smartphones and get their hands dirty. Still, thanks to our amazing team as well as our boss Oskar, who worked us hard but paid good money and still believed in the concept of work-life balance. Then, I looked forward to working almost every day of the year.

Over the past months, though, my diet had gotten out of whack. This last Christmas I'd taken overindulgence to a whole new level and I hadn't managed to get off the diet of having chocolate and other snacks the way I usually did. My increasing workload contributed to that: I've never been a breakfast type and during the day there were increasingly fewer opportunities to take a proper lunch break, leaving me no choice but to raid the fridge in the evenings. I've always been a hefty guy because I love food, and I'd grown even more since I met my girlfriend, Silke. I'd never forgotten the day we met five years ago: one of those days, she'd driven her Peugeot 206 into our garage for tuning, and her love for cars, her smile and most of all her curves had caught my fancy immediately.

A big girl herself, around 230 pounds on a 5'5" frame, Silke was my first partner that not only accepted but also appreciated my weight and even encouraged me to eat how much I wanted. She loved to grab and knead my belly or to pat my butt, even in public. Never indecently so but she was unashamedly obvious about the fact that she was into my body. Increasingly less so, though.

"You know I love that you're a big guy," she told me when she saw me raid the fridge after work the other day, "but please watch it, OK?"

It was the first time I noticed she was eyeing my body for anything but approval and it did not feel good. It was also the first time she'd ever criticized my weight. She never did so with anyone, not after what she had been through with her mom. After years of trying to please her and fighting her own weight, she'd finally embraced it. She'd been in a dark place and wouldn't ever go back. She always told me this with a grin, patting whatever part of me that was closest to her at the time. Lately, those parts of me got closer and closer, though, creeping onto and taking over her side of the bed. I was gaining fast, not only on my gut but also thighs and butt. I was becoming soft and doughy, not in any sight of a woman who preferred a mix of flab and muscle that she'd like to wake up to. That she would address my weight openly now told me the matter was serious.

So far, I hadn't thought so. I guess every big person has to make a decision at some point how much they let other people's comments and stares get to them. With my dad, I'd managed pretty quickly to let both bounce off, and meanwhile, I really couldn't give a damn what anyone else thought either. I'd so far brushed off my colleagues' ribbing, too. My best friend Lars, who I, unfortunately, got to see few weeks due to his busy job, also seemed a little worried the last time I saw him, but he didn't get on my case too much either.

"As long as you're healthy and happy with yourself," he told me, "it's your business. Just be careful, OK?"

"Hey," I grinned back at him, "I'd never let my-self get as big as those guys they have to lift out of their places with a crane."

It seemed I was well on my way, though. I did take Silke's words to heart but I just couldn't seem to break out of the pattern I'd fallen into. I kept gaining. I began to waddle. One day I felt a cool breeze on the underside of my belly and discovered with horror that the lowest part was peeking out. No, not just peeking: hanging. I was thirty-one only and already sagging! Due to my height, I already wore extra-long T-shirts and even those couldn't contain me anymore?

At work, it wasn't that much of a problem since we wore coveralls but even the 4XL ones I wore these days were having more and more trouble keeping me contained. My gut kept getting in the way, too, causing me to bump into and knock over things I couldn't see anymore. We had that little niche where we kept some of the tools and it began to be a pretty tight fit in there, as were the chairs whenever I went out for after-work drinks with the guys. I also had to sit down and rest more. My arms were getting heavy during overhead work.

I guess it was only a matter of time before Oskar, my boss, would call me into his cramped office, and one day in late spring he did. When I entered, he unfolded his gaunt body from his creaky chair, pushed some documents on the paper-strewn desk aside and sat on the edge as he usually did when he had something to discuss. He'd never been big on formality and we got along as if we were the same age even though he was close to 60. He motioned for me to have a seat on the old, sturdy round table in the corner and I carefully lowered myself onto it. I was grateful he hadn't suggested the chairs with the armrests.

"Blake," he began by wearing a frown and a worried look over the reading glasses he had pushed down on his long nose, "you're one of my best men but… your physique is becoming a problem."

Instantly I felt pale with the heat on my face. I have that skin type that's prone to blushing and I had never been good at hiding what I was thinking, and I usually never bother, but right now I wished I had one of those poker faces.

"I haven't had any complaints," Oskar went on in his gravelly voice and I suddenly had trouble concentrating on, "but I've observed some things and overheard others from the guys: you tire easily. You keep knocking things over or get stuck because you can't work in confined spaces anymore." He took off his glasses, twirling them in his long, cracked fingers. "Blake, I'm worried."

I didn't know when I'd last seen that particular look in his eyes and I wished it would go away.

"I know things have been getting out of hand," I finally managed to answer. I could hardly tell him that was due to stuffing myself at night after not being able to take a proper break during the day. That would sound really pathetic and it would come across as not being able to handle the workload. If I hoped to get a raise soon, I'd better shut up.

"Do you need some time off?" Oskar asked when I didn't continue. "I can't really spare you at the moment but if it would help, I could move some things around—"

Instantly I held up my hand, suddenly noticing how chubby it looked, especially in contrast to Oskar's. "No, it's fine. I want to be here."

"And I'm glad that you do." Still that worried look. I hated that look. "But if there is anything I can do, let me know, OK? You've got to get your weight under control. I would hate to lose you."

Lose me? I knew it was serious but 'lose me'? Suddenly not getting a raise sounded like the last thing I should worry about.

"You won't," I managed to tell him before I heaved myself to my feet again and Oskar clapped me on the shoulder, the sensation startling me for a moment. When had I developed so much back fat that Oskar's hand would cause ripples? Was it really that bad? I didn't feel bad. Sure, I got winded and tired more easily these days and I sweated more. Yeah, some tasks were becoming difficult to do but I could still handle my job.

When I reentered the work area, it felt as everyone was looking at me but nobody except for Olli, our first-year apprentice, who came up and asked what our talk had been about and telling me the others had guessed it already. Olli, on the other hand, attended trade school two days a week and hadn't witnessed all my little incidents and accidents. I managed to make up something believable and went back to work, my mind still snagged on something Oskar had said: he had 'overheard some things' from the guys. Had anyone snitched? No, I couldn't imagine that. We'd always been a great team and nobody had ever seemed to have a problem with my size. Or did they?

It was the first time I felt true panic. I had to get my weight under control. For God's sake, my job was on the line here and possibly my relationship, too. For a while now, Silke had stopped fondling me when we went out and I saw increasingly less action in bed either. She was on her feet a lot in her job and went speed-walking with friends twice a week, so she managed to keep her weight pretty stable. Watching me balloon in front of her eyes was not what she'd signed up for, nor was my possibly getting fired for being too fat.

I honestly meant to get a healthy dinner that night but somehow, I found myself leaning back in my easy chair again, the ruins of a gargantuan dinner on the tray before me. Silke's work day started and ended later than mine, so she wasn't home to witness it. I half-wished she would, though, and stop me. Still, no need to panic, I repeated to myself over and over that night and actually managed to pack a big but healthy sandwich and a banana the next day instead of getting a few bratwursts from across the street as usual. Of course, the guys gave me crap about it but that was alright. I, for one, felt proud of myself for eating nothing else during the day. Still, once I opened the fridge door that night, it was as if my growling stomach drowned out anything my conscience might have to say. No need to panic, I reminded myself again, one step at a time. First, I had to establish the pattern of eating a healthy lunch and then I'd take care of instituting a healthy dinner.

It didn't seem to be working, though. My pants kept getting tighter, as did my easy chair and even my beloved BMW 3 coupé. Since with all the extras it was worth a lot more than Silke's, I got to use the garage that came with the apartment while she parked on the curb. That garage was pretty narrow, though, so manoeuvring myself inside was always a mean feat because I couldn't open the door as far as I would have needed to. Also, my belly kept pushing against the steering wheel so I had to move the seat back more and more. Luckily my legs were long enough that I could still reach the pedals. Even so, it felt as if every few days I had to spread my legs more and more to accommodate my bulk.

And then it happened. One morning when I deposited my wide ass in the driver's seat and reached to pull the door shut, there was no bang. The door had bounced off my fat bulging over the driver's seat. My face felt as if it was going up in flames even though nobody else was around. I really needed to get my eating under control.

As it turned out, embarrassment wasn't enough of a motivator. The changes in my body were so gradual that I adjusted quickly and that the extra motion of bending towards the stick shift to keep my fat away from the door came naturally. Well, and then came the day when I found myself wedged between the stick shift and the door in a way that I couldn't move the stick anymore. Even though it had been a tight fit that morning, I had gotten to work OK, but now I was sitting in our company's parking lot, practically trapped. I had outgrown my car. Nobody who hadn't been there themselves could ever understand what that felt like. Freaking out would be an understatement. Not being able to walk very far or cycle at all, I depended on a set on wheels.

Somehow, I managed to shove some of my hip fat underneath and behind myself. It was anything but comfortable but at least I could drive now. As carefully as I could I took myself home, heaving a sigh of relief once I had yanked myself out of the car and closed the door behind me. Tomorrow I would have to borrow Silke's truck. Being an automotive enthusiast herself, one of the things I adored most about her, she loved powerful, comfortable cars. These days she drove a used Chevy S-10 pickup, a big-ass vehicle in the truest sense of the word. From the beginning, I'd been fascinated by the size of the twin globes that made up her ass but since she'd both put on weight along with me in the five years we'd been together, she'd upgraded. She still fit into my car but only her pickup's bench seat was able to accommodate that masterpiece comfortably, so we always took her truck when we went out together.

Well, and now I would have to ask her if we could swap for a while and hope she wouldn't suspect anything. I'd never been able to hide much from her. Even though I really needed to get serious about dropping some weight, right now I just needed to drop enough to fit back into my car. That shouldn't be too hard, should it? After all, only the day before I had fit, so it shouldn't take me more than a couple of days to get there again, right?

Wrong. I really tried this time but it seemed the more I tried, the more I gained. At some point, I couldn't come up with excuses for not driving my own car anymore and I had to come clean to Silke. Her face seemed to freeze over when I spilt the news that night on the couch, and she withdrew her hands when I reached out for them. It was the first time I had seen that face on her, and just like with Oskar, I hoped to never see it again.

"You can drive my pick up until you fit back into your car. Still," she folded her arms across her beautiful chest, giving me an ugly frown, "this is a wakeup call. You need to do something. I'll help you, you just need to tell me how. You need to want it yourself." She got up, her eyes piercing mine through her blue nerd frames. "Please, you *have* to do something. I… can't deal with this much longer."

And she shut herself in the bathroom. A moment later I heard water rushing into the tub. Did she actually mean to take a bath or was she trying to drown out the sound of her crying? Suddenly goose bumps broke out all over my arms. Of course, I had known Silke was unhappy with my weight but it was the first she hinted at a breakup. No, I just couldn't lose her. She was the best thing that had ever happened to me.

I tried, I really did this time but I just couldn't do it, and then the day came when Oskar called me into his office a second time and I knew it was over. The 1500€ angle grinder I had knocked off a workbench with my belly and destroyed the other day had been the final straw. He looked as crushed as I'd never ever seen him, only it was nothing compared to how I felt.

"I would give you a desk job but I know how hopeless you are with a computer," he told me while wearing a sick smile that did nothing to cheer me up. "Try to get healthy and take as long as you need. Your job is waiting for you; I can promise you that."

Normally Oskar would have to observe the legal notice period. In my case, the usual four weeks were extended to three months under German law since I had been a part of this company for eight years. When Oskar suggested instead I leave now and he'd pay me my full salary for one and a half month, I didn't argue, though. I had no more energy left to argue. Combined with my considerable overtime, I would leave now and still get paid for three months before the state's unemployment benefits would kick in. Still, it wouldn't even come to that. I might be the worst dieter on planet earth but I was great at my job and good mechanics were always in demand. It would be tough at my size but maybe there was a garage that had a spot for me. With my excellent references, I should be fine.

I wasn't. I really tried looking for a work and I actually got invited to a few interviews. Well, guess how those turned out. With every rejection letter, Netflix seemed like the better alternative to writing an application, as did the fridge, of course. Without a job, I moved less and ate more. As long as I went through ads and kept our place clean, Silke wasn't on my case too much but the more often she came home to me munching to some movie, with dishes and clothes strewn all over the apartment, the more I ticked her off. She'd always complained about having to clean up after me, but usually with good humour since I took care of everything that needed fixing. Now I wasn't taking care of anything anymore, though, least of all myself. My belly had surrendered to gravity and flowed over my lap. No T-shirt was large enough to cover it, so I had no choice but to tuck it into my ever-tightening pants. A salon visit was long overdue, too, but what for? Plus, I wouldn't fit into their chairs anyway. All in all, I couldn't blame Silke for staying on what remained, her side of the bed. I could see the train wreck ahead but I kept my eyes closed as if that could change reality.

Well, reality caught up with me a few days later: when a 4-week business trip came up for Silke, she gave me an ultimatum: clean up after myself and lose weight. If there was no visible progress, it was over and I was out. It was her place and most of the furniture was hers, too. When I'd moved out of my bachelor pad and into her place, I'd sold, given or thrown away most of my stuff since I hadn't treated it well anyway. I don't think I've ever cleaned my microwave once in the five years I've owned it.

The look Silke gave me before she left for her trip that morning finally seemed motivating enough. Again, I was wrong. After a promising start with some yoghurt and fruit for breakfast, I felt so ravenous by the time noon rolled around that I polished off two pizzas and a jar of ice-cream. I really tried to eat nothing for the rest of the day but when my growling stomach wouldn't let me sleep that night, I found myself in front of the fridge again. Now there was no one around to look decent for, I just cranked up the heat and spent all day in my oldest, baggiest briefs that didn't cut into my belly too much. Another benefit: no T-shirt meant no stains and no laundry.

You'd be surprised at how unaware you can be caught up onto becoming a whale. I didn't notice until the end of week three when I had a craving for Chinese food and decided to hit the buffet and I could n't fasten my jeans. I was so worried now, I tried my trusty sweatpants next. Silke, the always perfectly dressed and groomed, would kill me if she knew I planned to go out in sweats, and semi-clean ones at that, but she wasn't here to keep an eye on me. We did face time a lot but I always kept the phone aimed at my face and that hadn't changed since she left.

Like the jeans, my sweats were way tighter than they should have been. A nasty sense of foreboding hit me as I tried to pull my largest T-shirt down over my torso. No matter how much I kept tugging, it crept back up my sagging belly that hung over the rubber band of my briefs, covering a third of my thighs. I almost didn't dare breathe. Could somebody put on that much weight in such a short time? I needed to assess the full damage but Silke refused to keep a scale at our place, let alone a heavy-duty model for up to 500 lbs. Since that was close to what I might be looking at. Measuring it was then. Hastily, I went through Silke's closet for her sewing stuff, throwing things left and right until I finally found the 60" tape measure. I sat down on the bed, not letting my belly sag down between my thighs as usual but balancing the full bulk on top of them. I trapped one end of the tape measure between two fat rolls and struggled to wind the rest around my back and belly. Not a chance. There was no way for me to reach around myself, and judging by the remaining length of the tape, the ends wouldn't even reach!

This couldn't be happening. How could I have let things get so out of hand? With no one there to force me out of the apartment for a walk or a trip to the store, I had stayed inside and ordered in, not noticing that I was steadily outgrowing everything. Silke had demanded visible progress, and by God was it visible. I must have gained another twenty pounds in the time she was gone!

Think, I kept repeating to myself. The first step was the clothes. With no exact measurements, I had no choice but to order a few shirts, T-shirts and pants in 8XL, two of them with those loser elastic waistbands, just in case. Since I'd checked 'overnight delivery', everything arrived the next day. The shirts and T-shirts fit OK width-wise but even their extra length couldn't cover my sagging belly. The only option I had was to stuff it into my pants, meaning that with this extra girth only the two pairs of jeans with the elastic waistband fit. The result looked terrible and there was no doubt Silke would think so, too.

I got rip-roaring drunk that night. In the morning, food was the only thing to battle the hangover from hell, and in this manner one day blurred into the next. It was no wonder I forgot which time Silke was supposed to be back from her trip and it didn't help that the apartment was a mess either. I don't think I've ever heard someone scream as loudly and as long as Silke did. I'd heard all those words before "lazy", "pig", "loser", "no self-respect", but never from her, and never within a few seconds at that many decibels. I took the verbal beating until the words "Look at yourself. You're a waste of space, literally. A whole lot of space wasting."

I did look down myself. Actually, wherever I turned I saw myself. It was impossible not to. My gut, competing for space with moobs that probably needed a cup size DD, was always the first thing to enter a room. My arms, flabbily rolls, stuck out because they rested on the giant fat pads under my upper arms. When I sat, I saw ass cheeks to my left and right that invaded half the couch. I also felt myself all the time. My thighs rubbing each other, my upper-arm flab jiggling or my outlying regions wobbling when I walked or turned. There was no movement that didn't lead to other movements.

How could I have let this happen? It wasn't as if I'd woken up fat, I'd been there for every bite, watching myself grow. Except I hadn't watched. Somehow, I'd shut out the unobstructed. I had turned into a disgusting whale, barely capable of wiping his own ass anymore, let alone get a job. I was a freaking waste of space. Mutely I turned and trudged out, Silke's words ringing in my ears that she would toss in the trash whatever I didn't pick up by the end of the week.

Only the first gust of frigid air told me I was outside of our apartment building. My own panting all but drowned out the sounds of cars and people as I realized how long it had been since I had walked further than from the couch to the kitchen or to the bedroom. Feeling my gut slap against my thighs with every laborious step, I stumbled forward, people's disgusted or incredulous looks hitting me left and right. Suddenly, a bus stopped and opened its doors with its hissingly signature, spewing out more gawking people. Blindly I entered and thrust a few coins at the gaping elderly driver before I turned to the left and discovered I wouldn't fit through the turnstile. My face in flames, I kept my head down as I lumbered back outside and reentered through the rear door, causing the other passengers to either stare or look away in disgust, the nearest of them wrinkling their noses at my drunk and un-showered presence.

Despite the growing exhaustion in my legs I only dared sit when almost everyone had left the bus. At last, it pulled up to the curb at its last stop, a small carpool-and-commute parking lot at the edge of the woods close to the Autobahn. I didn't know why but I got off and stumbled on, not stopping until I found myself sagging against the sodden parapet of a concrete bridge.

It couldn't have taken more than a few seconds to reflect on my way from fat but I was happy to be a homeless, jobless whale. Well, and that's how long it would take to make that whale disappear. They may say alcohol messed with your senses but I had never seen clearer in my entire life. I braced both hands on the wet, mossy concrete of the parapet and tried to push myself up. And again. Not a chance, not with such a monster wearing a gut in the way. I tried again, already out of breath. Next, I turned and tried to heave myself up, ass first. Not working either. Not only was the rail in the way, but also the parapet was just too high, impossible to tackle for a guy like me. The simple fact was that I was too fat to live but also too fat to die. When I realized that I couldn't even finish *this* job, I felt my knees buckle and slumped onto the frozen ground.

CHAPTER TWO

Ela: My watch

"Would you like to go in front of me?"

The short, acne-riddled man in his late twenties blushed and dipped his head, only to raise it briefly again in a grateful nod before his slight figure sidled past my overfull cart. Although the few and unhealthy purchases that his small hands placed on the checkout belt at Aldi's bespoke a bachelor, I had learned from extensive people-watching that a seemingly lonely nerd may leave a grocery store and kiss his awaiting beautiful partner and adorable kid. Or that an old gent bent over his cane would withdraw a smartphone newer than my own, record two fighting sparrows and share the video over on WhatsApp. Or that a traditionally dressed Muslim sometimes spoke with the thick regional dialect that still eluded me after three years of living here due to lack of daily exposure. Never assume anything about anyone, I had to learn quickly. People assumed things about me, too, and they couldn't be more wrong.

While I transferred the contents of my carefully packed cart onto the belt, my peripheral vision reported that the shy customer in front of me had half-turned to look at me while two youngsters ahead of him were piecing together the amount for their considerable amount of sugar-laden snacks. Textbook munchies. The shy man's eyes were still on me, probably wondering why anyone would wear only a thin turtleneck instead of a thick jacket in this weather. Well, when gloves and other sartorial means of shielding oneself are a year-round necessity, it gets rather warm, so I always left my padded coat in the car. Offering the man, a fleeting but sufficiently distant smile so he wouldn't feel hurt but not get his hopes up either, I proceeded by loading the supplies onto the belt that would last me for the next month.

"Are- are you planning a party?" the man ventured, at last, his eyes struggling to stay on mine once I had straightened and faced him.

"No."

Again, I took care to pair my answer with a token smile so as not to wound him. I had learned the hard way that a failed attempt at flirtation can hurt more than the person on the dispensing end of the rebuff may believe. I continued to empty my cart, the man's eyes still on me but his mouth quiet now. Hopefully, he would turn back around soon. Suddenly a lady in her late thirties with a bulging cotton bag in one and a pre-school-aged girl, on the other hand, stepped behind me, causing me to edge past my shopping cart as quickly as I could. My change in location might trigger more undue hope in the shy man but the protective distance to a child was vital. Children were prone to sudden, uncontrolled movements.

Indeed, the man turned over his shoulder again, offering an endearing smile but I kept my gaze on my booted feet, listening to his brief greet-pay-and-pack process. I only looked up when it was my turn, catching one last hopeful look from the man as he turned to leave. I did offer one in return but the one of the distant stranger I was and would most likely be for the rest of my life.

3D-puzzling a month's worth of supplies back into a shopping cart took a while, and by the time I pulled out my debit card, I had worked up a fine sheen of sweat. Thankfully I would be able to remove my thin gloves in the car. It had taken some time to find this pair that was tight, of a pleasant material and that allowed enough tactility. At last, the transaction was complete and I smiled at the cashier before I leaned into the cart with my full but inconsequential weight to propel it forward.

"Uh, excuse me?"

I registered the child's voice only dimly and kept on walking. Only a few more steps to the car, several minutes to transfer my cart's contents into the trailer and then I was off. No accidents this time. A tap on my elbow caused me to whirl around, the remainder of my thoughts scattering like the dry leaves outside. It was the little girl that had stood behind me, with her fine reddish-blond hair and adorable glasses with butterflies on them. Apparently, she had worn a wide smile on those chubby cheeks before I'd startled and scared her.

"I... I'm sorry, I didn't mean to scare you," the impossibly polite girl mumbled in a sweet voice and sought comfort in her butterfly snow boots for a moment. Then she brightened again. "But this fell out of your cart."

Her chubby hand held up a pack of cleaning rags that had apparently fallen out of my overstuffed cart. I knew I shouldn't but that kid looked so open and sweet that I just had to squat and smile at her, my gloved fingers brushing hers as I accepted the rags from her.

"I didn't mean to startle you either, sweetheart," I told her in a low, gentle voice that seemed to restore her to her former sparkling self. "Thank you very much, that was really nice of you."

"You're welcome."

I couldn't help it, I remained on the ground. Her cute face was simply irresistible. Now her small hand stretched out again, pointing to my head.

"I like your spirals."

"Thank you." Most of my hair reached down to the clasp of my bra but the right side of my head was shaven down to a fraction of an inch. From time to time I used a small, special shaver to experiment with new patterns. The girl's eyes remained riveted to my hair.

"Did you do them yourself?"

"Yes, I did."

"They are so pretty. May I touch them?" Not waiting for an answer, her chubby fingers zoomed in on their target. Instinctively I pulled back, scrambling back to my feet. I heard a sharp intake of breath and again the little face lowered. "Sorry."

I might not know if my scalp would be as harmful to people like the rest of my skin but I was not going to make this adorable kid my guinea pig. What would I have given to feel her small fingers on my scalp, to breathe in her child scent and to perhaps graze her silky skin, but it was impossible. I would most likely never touch a child again, much less have one of my own. I would never have what was required to make children either, nor the special someone to make them with. The only thing that remained in my power was to console the hurt child in front of me before I sought refuge in my solitude again.

"It's not your fault," I gently told the girl, whose eyes remained downcast, "I just don't like to be touched. Some people are just not as open as you are." The little head rose and a pair of green eyes a shade lighter than my own made careful contact. "You'll find out over time with whom it's OK to touch and with whom it isn't." I swallowed reflexively as I felt my throat close up. "I... I have to go now. Thank you for this."

I lifted the packet of rags and sent one last smile the girl's way before I moved away from her, tears already stinging in my eyes. I stored my purchases in the trailer more haphazardly than was my usual fashion and hurriedly secured the tarp, all the while aware of my fellow shoppers' curious gazes at me and the supplies and from their gazes, I knew they would be thinking about what a single woman in her early thirties might do with these many supplies. As long as they only stared, though, everyone would stay safe. With a grateful sigh, I sank into the driver seat at last and pulled the door shut to ward off the icy rain into which the snow had turned a minute ago.

My breath was forming small clouds and I cranked up the AC as soon as I had turned the key. As always, I directed all of my concentration on driving and pulled out of the parking lot carefully. I couldn't afford accidents. The encounter with the little girl had been a close one already. Usually, I moved through the masses like a drop of oil on water but some minor accidents invariably happened, and only by feigning utter ignorance had I extricated myself from the situation. How long my condition would last or whether I would at least find an "emulsifier" one day was no longer the first thought I woke up to and the last one I took to bed with me but it was always there, sometimes watching from afar or hovering close by.

No, it wouldn't do to dwell on my gloomy prospects; I had to be grateful for the small blessings: I owned a fully paid small house and enjoyed a steady stream of income, unconventional though the source was. Everything I had to handle in person was in driving distance and for anything else I enjoyed a strong and reliable internet connection, courtesy of a nearby radio mast.

Finding that house had been a tinge of luck. Despite its good condition, a one-storey home in a remote location in a sparsely populated area did not attract many buyers and I had snatched it up for a song while my condo in the centre of Frankfurt had sold for three times more. Due to the low wage level in this area, the cost for some minor repairs and the replacement of the tub with a walk-in shower had been affordable as well, so, all in all, I was not only debt-free but had some savings left over. Yes, those were good thoughts. Just a few more of those and perhaps there was a chance the face of that little girl wouldn't follow me to bed tonight.

The rain was pelting down harder now. Most people believe Germany to be arctic all year round whereas millions of heat-scorched lawns and miniskirts in many parts of the country beg to differ between June and August. However, certain areas are, in fact, afflicted with more protracted periods of hibernal temperatures, such as this one, which made it perfect for my needs as it necessitated protective clothing. I could have done without the considerable amounts of precipitation but after three years in this area I was used to it, and so was my trusty minivan that tackled each mile towards my isolated house with 4WD confidence.

At last I reached the small concrete bridge that ultimately led to an uphill trail from which another narrow, almost invisible path branched off towards my house. Only a few minutes more and I would be home, safe and sound. Unloading the supplies could wait until the rain had abated. Suddenly I caught a movement from the corner, something big and grey that seemed to slump, although that was practically impossible to tell when the world was shrouded in liquid grey curtains. Nonetheless, I activated my hazard lights and stepped on the brake with caution, grateful for my high-quality tires. What was that big, indistinguishable mass? It didn't look like a living creature and yet I had seen it move. Suddenly it shifted again. Oh God, this was definitely a human hand.

My decision was made within a fraction of a second: as big a threat as I may be to that person, the cold posed the bigger one. A mere ten minutes on the cold ground could render them so weak and immobile they would never be able to get up again. Once I had shrugged into my padded raincoat, scarf, hat and gloves, I carefully made my way to the sodden mass on the ground.

Lying on his right side in front of me was the biggest man I had ever laid eyes on in real life. The clingy fabric of his drenched grey leather jacket and jeans outlined his flesh and shaped like a haphazardly stuffed cushion. His calves looked larger than my thighs and his thighs, wider than my torso. His belly lay as though poured out of him as a viscous mass and the hand that peeked out from one of the sleeves was chubby like a toddler's. The man's face was obscured by the hood of his sweatshirt. The unexpected presence of this even more unexpected trembling shape caused me to swallow reflexively and my lower belly to… good question, what was my lowered belly doing? No, whatever it was, my priority was the man in front of me. I bent.

"Hello? Hello, can you hear me?"

A startled twitch interrupted the trembling but there was no reply. I squatted and leaned closer.

"Can you hear me?"

Still, there was no verbal reaction. Panic strangled me from within. Since I couldn't possibly carry a man of his size, I would have to call an ambulance if he didn't respond. The last thing I needed was to have my contact details in the hands of a medical authority. Now the man's head slowly lifted, offering a visible access to his round cheeks; a double chin having what looked too scraggy and haphazard to be an intentional beard. A smallmouth in the midst of the scruff opened, his lips trembling like the rest of his massive body, but still, no sound emerged.

"You need to get out of the cold. Do you think you can get up?"

Still, nothing, there was still no verbal response. Perhaps he didn't understand German? I repeated my words in English, French and I was just about to piece together my meagre Spanish when his lips opened again.

"M- maybe I c- can but I w- won't."

The rush of relief I felt at hearing German words, lightly tinged with the local dialect, the ones the man had chosen to utter, pierced me to the core. I had been there myself, and although on some days I wished I could have gone through with it because there were still people to whom I still meant something. As wrapped up in oneself as a suicidal person might be, their life – and death – affected others. I could not let him die, and that meant getting him out of the cold fast. Every minute was a risk.

"Do you want to die?" I challenged the man whose head had turned back to the ground. Now it turned again and his eyes fixed themselves on mine with determination.

"Yes."

"Well, too bad because I'm here now and you're not going to die on my watch."

"And wh-what are you g-going to do, c-carry me?" he scoffed, his grimaced smile revealed his straight teeth. For some reasons, it didn't look quite like the way teeth were supposed to. I pushed that observation aside. At least, his sense of humour hadn't fallen prey to hypothermia yet.

"No, I was counting on your cooperation."

"N- not going to happen." His head turned again.

I straightened, unsheathing my ultimate weapon. "Then you leave me no other choice but to call an ambulance. And the police, just in case."

Loath though I was to turn this spot into an ought-to-be crime scene and to become involved with the authorities, I was prepared to do so as a last resort. Within the past three years, I had compiled an arsenal of evasion and unobtrusiveness techniques and stood a good chance at extricating myself from the situation undetected. The sight of the man in front of me, however, assured me that we would be spared from any third-party involvement after all. With visible reluctance the hood-covered head lifted and its owner laboriously shifted himself into a sitting position, his copious flesh undulating and resettling. I knew I shouldn't stare but couldn't help it, nor could I keep my lower anatomy by commenting on the sight in front of me. No, no, no, no! I had felt the sensation before, and as inappropriate as it had been then, it was nothing compared to this. The man was suicidal and suffering from hypothermia! At last, I managed to shake myself out of the bewildering trance.

"Atta boy."

I was treated to another noise of derision before the man began to pull himself to his feet by the aid of the concrete parapet, a spectacle to behold with his bulges shifting and resifting until finally settling into what must be their accustomed places. I never realized how much flesh the human body could hold, and even with his impressive height of about 6'3" visually balancing out his mass, he had to be at least three times the weight of a normal person. He was panting heavily. With his weight but also his scruff and cheeks caked in dirt he appeared of indeterminable age. A little older than me possibly, late thirties?

"And wh- what are you g- going to d- do with me now, huh?" he panted, most likely intending to glower down at me. With my height of 6'1", however, the preposition 'down' hardly applied, so I stared right back despite my intensifying discomfort in my lower belly. I'm the biggest threat there is, buddy, so save yourself the wrinkles and stop glaring. The thought actually helped to tune out my unbidden bodily reaction and to let reason take over.

"Take you to my place."

His scowl morphed into a narrow-eyed stare. "Wh- why?"

"Duh, to get you dry?"

His stare continued. "You w- want to take a d- dirty, d- drenched, super f- fat stranger to your p- place?"

"Yes."

One of the few perks of my condition was that I never had to fear for my safety. Should the man turn out to be an unsavoury character and choose to act on his perversions, he would regret his decision the second his thing touched my skin. On the bright side, it would be the last time he'd unzipped his pants for that purpose. Until he was proven guilty, however, I would do my best to get him back on his feet, meaning that we had no time for Q and A.

"Did you drive here?"

He shook his head, a needless waste of energy when hypothermia was taking care of the shaking already. "B- bus."

Good, at least I wouldn't have to worry about moving not only him but also his vehicle.

"I w- won't fit in the passenger seat, y- you know," the man's snarl punctured my little bubble of optimism.

"Then get in the rear," I snapped at him, fed up with his lack of cooperation. I had hurt enough people and it was time I helped someone. After some more staring, albeit with his eyes at a less hostile aperture, he shifted his impossibly thick thighs at last and slowly made his lumbering way over to my van. A few long strides took me past him easily and I opened the sliding door, climbing inside and rearranging the purchases inside, transferring some onto the passenger seat, before I spread out a blanket I always kept in the car. Was he really too big to sit in front? Instantly I felt the heat in my cheeks.

Again, I shifted my thoughts towards the logistics at hand. My van will be able to handle the extra load, even though the weight of the trailer and supplies. Thank God for strong engines and the lack of rear windows so no one would notice I was transporting a person. There, space should be sufficient. I climbed back out, only to catch him watching me from where he was holding on to the side panel, trembling and panting.

"Can you get in?"

He only scowled and I stepped aside. His face morphed into a grimace as the van dipped to the right but at last, he slumped down on the blanket and the weight distribution was even once more. Certain I had schooled my features into submission and wouldn't add facially to his discomfiture, I turned to face him again.

"All set?" He only scowled again in response and I slid the door shut.

A moment later we were rolling and the added weight already discernible as I worked on the pedals. Now that the wind, which had been blowing away from the man, had been replaced by an enclosed space, my nostrils cringed under the onslaught of the signature smell of an unwashed person. Oh Lord! what kind of man had I scraped off the road? One that was best dealt with while breathing through my mouth only, that's for sure. Only a minute could have passed but already the silence was bearing down on me – quite ironic since silence was the default sound of my world. The flesh on the man's broad back quivered not only from the cold but with every pothole, too.

"C- could you c- crank up the heat?"

"Changed your mind about death then?"

I just couldn't stop myself. I needed to prick and poke him to keep him alert and focused on living. If anyone knew, it was me. I cranked up the heat to the max and the silence wore on. All the way up the small incline that led to the deserted road with the patchy pavement, I willed my vehicle to convey us back to my house, even with the considerable extra cargo. At last, I turned into the narrow gravel turnoff shrouded by trees. Only the package-deposit box hinted at a human presence but with my having painted them in a dark green, only the mail carriers were aware of their existence.

My house was a one-storey building with a shallow roof and it never had a basement, only 750 square feet, sitting next to a garage of almost two-thirds its size. Usually I would unload the trailer, detach it and tuck it safely into the garage along with the car but for now, that could wait. Nothing would perish in this cold anyway. After I had opened the door, I hurried through the arctic rain to unlock the front door. By the time I squelched my way back to the car, the man was just transferring his weight to his feet, all the while holding on to the car. The pallor of his face was alarming.

"Do you think you can make it to the door?"

"Wh- what's the- alternative?"

He didn't wait for an answer but started lumbering forward. After closing and locking the car, I easily caught up with him. "The bathroom is at right-end of the two doors straight ahead. I'm going to get you some towels," I threw my shoulder over as I hurried inside, watching him lift his legs up the two concrete steps. In my bedroom where I kept the big towels I hardly used, I stacked three of the largest on one arm, already preoccupied in what he would dress himself during the one and a half hour; the washing machine and the dryer would require to provide him with dry, clean clothing again.

A trail of muddy, wet prints was glaring at me more than a trunkful of giant fluorescent arrows would, and only by remembering the current state of their author did I stifle the urge to communicate my barbarity vociferously to him. Well, should he commit another hygienic offence when he was warmed up, I wouldn't spare him, I promised myself when I joined him in the bathroom. I had always thought it was spacious enough but that his presence made look positively cramped. If at all possible, he was shaking more than before, sending his massive flesh wobbling around. He was eyeing my capacious walk-in shower with a blend of gratefulness and disbelief, and at that moment, I felt grateful myself that his size coincided with my preference for showers over baths. When you're a tall person, one part of you inevitably sticks out of the tub and turns cold.

"You can wash your clothes while you shower," I told him while I filled in detergent and chose the right program. "Just push this button and if your clothes are dryer-safe, put them in here and turn this knob." He nodded. "You can take as long as you want. This house is connected to the normal water and sewer system, so there is no need to ration. In the meantime, I'm going to look for something you can wear."

"Y- yeah, g- good luck with that," he stuttered behind me. I heard that over my shoulder before I practically bolted and pushed the door shut behind me, drawing what felt like my first deep breath in the past ten minutes.

Although the saying goes that 'Karma is a bitch,' I had learned the hard way that she only is if you are, and she certainly thought the opportunity had come for more payback: out of all people she had to throw a morbidly obese man my way. I had certainly ridiculed enough of them to deserve an atonement for my sins this way, but did it have to be one in such a precarious frame of mind? He wanted to take his own life and I was responsible for him now – me of all people who shouldn't be given responsibility for a tortoise. What would make this man want to commit suicide? His weight possibly but not definitely factored in. Why had he come out here of all places? Was anyone looking for him?

An intensifying heat alerted me to the fact that I was still wearing my coat, hat and gloves. Quickly, I dropped everything with the gloves in their places. I cranked up the heat and began to make tea. I needed to keep the man warm even after his shower, and I could stand a mug as well. Then I tackled the impossible task of procuring clothes in his size. The best substitute for a sweater turned out to be a black fringed poncho interwoven with fine golden threads – not exactly manly but he would have to suck it up. My size-twelve woollen socks should fit him but what would I do for pants? Well, he would have no other chance but to safety-pin two woollen blankets together and wrap them around himself. Just as I emerged from my bedroom with the makeshift clothes, I heard the shower stop, a circumstance on which my lowered anatomy chose to comment instantly. Clenching my thighs together and squeezing my eyes shut as if that could ward off the inexplicable sensation, I knocked on the door.

"Uh-huh," it suddenly hit me that I didn't even know his name, "I have a poncho that should fit you but I didn't have anything for pants beside pinned-together blankets. I'm setting everything outside the bathroom door."

No answer. I fled back into the open kitchen/dining/living area to take out the tea bags before I turned towards my small, rectangular wooden table and was presented with another obstacle: there was no way my standard-size chairs could accommodate his heft. The couch would but one of my self-enforced rules of living alone was never to mix locations and functions. A couch was for lounging and a table was for food and drink. Eating meals on the couch in front of the TV is often the first step of letting yourself go as a single, which eventually leads to a greasy-haired, stained-bathrobe-clad existence in front of the TV. Well, for now, there was no other option, I sighed inwardly and carried the tray to the couch table at the other end of the rectangular room, after which I placed a big pot with water for a broth on the stove. Suddenly, I heard the bathroom lock click and the sound shuffled. There was no more putting off the confrontation. I quickly slipped my gloves back on that I had stuffed into the back pocket of my jeans and turned to face my guest.

I was facing a possibly 500-pound man, his skin crimson red from the shower, at least those parts that weren't covered in my poncho and the blankets around his tummy – let's call it 'waist' for simplicity. A plump and dimpled hand kept the fabric in place. Chubby wouldn't begin to describe his Michelin-man-like arms protruding from under the poncho. His eyes, reflecting something between mortification and murder, dared me to laugh. His eye colour was indistinguishable from my distance but now I could see that his face was round and that he possessed dark hair with a bit of curl in dire need of a trim. His nose was nothing out of the ordinary and his mouth small and soft-looking with a pronounced double chin underneath. All in all, I was staring into a likeable face despite his scraggly beard and scowl. I mentally corrected my guess from end to mid-thirties.

Again, I squeezed my eyes shut against the onset of tingles and treated myself to another breath before I looked at him again. "Sit. Have some tea. I've prepared a broth, too."

The man eyed the couch as if assessing its strength but finally lowered himself on the longer part of the L-shape, carefully holding the blankets together over his spreading bulk. Averting my face in order to conceal my reddening cheeks and to spare him any more embarrassment, I took a seat on my cherished brown sheepskin on the shorter end of the couch. Out of the corner of my eye, I saw the man pick up his mug and gradually he seemed to relax a bit.

Running my fingertips over the fuzziness of the sheepskin brought a smile to my face as always. I might not be able to touch human skin but I always made the most out of the connection with certain inorganic materials. A sharp gasp brought my gaze up to the man, who had just burnt his tongue on the hot tea. For a moment he looked as adorable as a child, an impression emphasized by his round cheeks and chubby hands. He deposited the offending item back on the couch table and met my eyes at last.

"Thanks."

More so than the single word it was his face which betrayed the extent of his gratefulness.

"You're welcome."

"What's your name?" he asked, never taking his gaze off me.

"Ela. And yours?"

"Blake."

It was an American name, was it not? Now, however, was not the time to discuss personal details. Again, we both stared at each other. The longer I was exposed to this man's presence, the more acutely my mind and body reminded me of how long it had been since I had faced and conversed with a person in such proximity.

"Are you feeling better?"

"I'm no longer cold."

The omission implied that the mental state he was in had hardly improved. He needed to be kept safe. "Is there anyone you'd like to call?"

"No." His mood, rather neutral so far, now seemed to cast its own shadow. "I'll just wait for my clothes to wash and dry and then I'll be out of your hair."

I cast a sceptical look out the window. "I doubt that. If anything, it's getting worse. You should stay until it's over."

He followed my gaze out the window. "That could take all night."

"Then you may spend the night." Whoops! As little as I had meant to extend the invitation, at that moment I realized that I meant it.

His eyes accosted to mine again, now narrowed with suspicion. "Why are you doing this?" His incredulity morphed into a sneer. "Haven't your parents told you not to speak to strangers, let alone let them shower or spend the night at your place?"

I couldn't suppress a wince at the mention of a mother I might never see again but managed to change the wince into a shrug. "I'm a grown-up."

"I still don't get it," the large man named Blake declared, at last, his eyes still on me.

"That's OK."

When it became an evidence that I wouldn't elaborate it to him, his gaze dropped to my hands. "Why are you wearing gloves?"

"Because I can," I replied him succinctly.

I had come to find out that monosyllabic and information-deprived answers disconcerted people to such an extent that they usually didn't probe any deeper. We continued to sip our tea in silence until I heard the water in the pot on the stove bubble and I hopped up in relief.

"Would you like some hot broth?"

For a moment he looked caged. "That sounds good," he replied at last. "Uh-huh, do you have a hairdryer so I can dry my shoes in the meantime?"

"Sure. In the cabinet under the sink."

"Thanks."

I didn't stay to watch him heave himself to his feet. My body couldn't take much more of this… this vicarious embarrassment, that's what this tingle had to be. Five minutes later I carried the broth with egg and some alphabet noodles over to the couch table and turned on some music in order to fill the silence that was sure to follow. At that moment I heard the hairdryer stop and Blake reemerged from the bathroom, the sight of his massive shape causing my insides to twist into knots again, even more so when he antagonized the pins that held the blankets together by gingerly lowering himself once more.

Averting my face again, I concentrated on the act of placing one of my round wooden plates on my lap to balance the soup bowl on before I handed another one to Blake. At that moment I realized that it would be impossible for him to follow suit as he had to spread his thighs wide to accommodate his enormous belly. One of the few advantages of my condition was that all this time spent removed from people had sharpened my heretofore nonexistent perception of their needs. With a warm face, I withdrew my hand again and held out the tray to him instead, not meeting his eyes. Again, we consumed the liquid in front of us without conversation until we were both full and dared to face one another.

"You don't have to talk about it, you know, but just in case you do, I'll listen."

He laughed with more surprise than humour. "It's a long story. Something you shouldn't trigger your concern on. I'll be out of here first thing in the morning anyway. I'll have a cab pick me—"

The remainder of his utterance drowned in a massive gulp.

"You don't have enough money with you, do you?" I probed softly after a moment during which his cheeks had turned pink.

"No." He swallowed again. "And in case you are about to offer me a drive, please don't."

"To quote you, what's the alternative?" Silence. "If I drive you home, will there be someone waiting for you?"

Blake gritted his funny-looking teeth and said nothing while I felt my own teeth sink into my lower lip, a habit I had thought long broken but that I had evidently engaged just not in lately, for lack of opportunity. No, I wouldn't pry any further. He clearly didn't want to share, and prodding him would come across as pushy if not outright weird. I had done for him what I could, and yet, I heard myself blurt before I managed to snatch back the words by their collar:

"I don't feel comfortable leaving you by yourself."

This time his chuckle was devoid of all humour. "Don't worry, I don't think I'll find a beam strong enough to hang myself from and I won't be able to slit my wrists off either since I would never get the razor blade through all this fat." He lifted his chubby arm, his visible upper arm flabbily dangled, while his eyes challenged mine to comment.

Although my tongue did not, other parts of my body certainly did, and I clamped my thighs shut again before I got up to both cleanup and put my unsuspecting tormentor out of my sight. It was of no use. I could feel his eyes on me the entire time I spent carrying the dishes over to the kitchen area. At last, I was able to exhale a few loud breaths over the sound of water rushing into the big pot in the sink. Suddenly I felt the back of my neck prickle with Blake's presence, realizing that: I hadn't heard him get up over the sound of the running water and my lower arms and hands were exposed because I had pushed up my sleeves. I whirled around in panic, shielding my hands behind my back.

"Ela? I'm sorry, I— "

I jumped when I saw him step closer. He might not even have meant to touch me but I could never be too careful. Even though Blake's round face shuttered at once, I briefly caught the pain in his eyes I now knew to be a blend of blue and green.

"No, *I'm* sorry— "

He held up a plump palm. "Don't bother, I get it."

He retreated back to the bathroom, presumably to check on the progress of his clothes. His wide hips roughly brushed the doorway. If my cheeks felt warm before, they positively went up in flames at the sight. Then Blake returned, his clothes probably in the dryer now, not meeting my eyes. I wished I could explain my reaction to him but there was no way.

"I assume you'll put me up on the couch tonight, right?" he grumbled, barely looking at me. I only nodded. "Just point me to the closet with the sheets and I'll take care of it. You've done more than enough."

It didn't feel like a compliment. With one frightened jump, I had destroyed the bit of trust I thought had blossomed between us, and possibly his will to live, too. He wasn't my responsibility but I needed to leave a mark on this world that wasn't a blister or a scar. He needed to stay alive.

"The bedding is in my bedroom. I'll get it."

Blake accepted the bedding from me without much a thank you, and although, I tried to make myself busy by doing the dishes, I couldn't help but glance over my shoulder occasionally. He'd pulled back the low table in order to unfold the couch, huffing as he bent over the massive rolls that formed his mid-section while taking care to hold the blankets in place. Unable to bear the sight of his quivering mass and the sound of his laboured breathing any longer, I hastily finished up the dishes and fled to the bathroom.

A splash and a cold sensation in my thick pairs of socks brought me up short: Blake had positively flooded the bathroom floor, plus left his towel on the floor in a sodden heap. The hair dryer was still sitting on the sink, and instantly a haze of emotional confusion lifted. Although I managed to lay out a toothbrush for the violator of basic human cleanliness, that was where my role as a gracious hostess stopped. After I had mopped up the floor, wrung out and hung the towel, I marched back into the living area. Even making allowances for his state of mind and hypothermia, his manners had been nothing but lacking, even after he had recovered from the worst. Although he had only been in my carefully ordered life for two hours, I already felt undone.

"You know; the least you can do when you're in somebody else's house is be neat. You don't flood other people's bathrooms or drop their towels on the flooded floor, and you always at least *offer* to take off your shoes before entering. And *that* is no way to make a bed either!" I finished my heated tirade with a contemptuous look at the mess on the couch.

I glared at the astonished-looking man until he moved aside and I could tuck in the corners of the bed sheet neatly and shake the duvet in its case so it didn't bunch up on one side and remain empty on the other. I garnished my work with another scowl and just when he opened his mouth, I messed everything up again. "Now you do it."

My chin stayed up until he complied, looking surprised at himself. Again, he struggled with the task of bending over but finished at last.

"There you go! There's a fresh toothbrush for you in the bathroom. Good night," I said to him and indeed, it turned out to be a goodnight henceforth.

CHAPTER THREE
Blake: Hell

Most people tossed and turned when they couldn't sleep. If I did, I would wreck even this high-quality couch, and so I carefully shifted my dense body, feeling my fat slosh around. One would think someone with as much padding would have no trouble finding a comfortable position. Well, they'd be wrong. Lying on my back had been out of the question for years as I couldn't breathe properly with my own weight pressing down on my lungs, and in all other positions, I had to rearrange myself constantly so I wouldn't lie on my own flesh. If you haven't been there, you don't get it. Believe it or not, being fat, even super fat, isn't so bad as long as you're healthy, a productive member of society and have a cute partner. Not having or being either, it was hell. I had myself to blame for it but it was hell nonetheless. I'd lied when I'd told Ela it was a long story how I'd ended up at the bridge. In fact, it was as short as being wretched: I ate myself into a whale size, got kicked out and wanted to end it all.

That strange girl with the as strange as fitting name Ela had gone out of her way to help a blubbery mountain of a stranger who had done nothing but snarl at her and dirty her previously germ-free home. She'd probably saved my life. If I'd lain on the freezing ground for much longer, I wouldn't have been able to get up even if I'd wanted to. This part of the woods probably saw one car per day, if any. Well, and today it had been hers. She'd taken action and not let my whining put her off nor pestered me with questions. In fact, except for my name and if there was somebody I wanted to call the woman with skin as pale as her name hadn't asked me anything.

She looked like a veritable Snow-white with that skin, her jet-black hair and the red lips she kept gnawing whenever she felt uncomfortable. What was different from the fairy tale was her impressive height, the slight gap between her front teeth and her buzzed hair on the right side with spirals shaven into it. She was one hot package and yet she had looked at and treated me like a person, an equal. She hadn't seemed put off by my size the way skinniest people were, at least not until I'd gotten too close to her. Yeah, I was a freak show but I had never made anyone jump like that. I had seen the actual fear in her cat-green eyes. What did she think I was going to do? Up until she'd flinched, I hadn't even planned on touching her. Well, at least not with my hands. These days I was barely able to stand close to someone without my body touching them.

Why did it feel like I had screwed up when I'd cut her off instead of listening to her explanation? I mean, surely it couldn't have been anything but my weight that had made her jump, and did I have to listen to that? Hell, no. Still, I should have known better than to snap at my rescuer like that. And now she was lying one room away, probably wondering if the tub of lard would wreck her couch. No, somehow that image of her didn't fit:

She had offered the couch to me instead of a chair.

She had exchanged the wooden plate for a tray that I could be balanced on my lap.

That girl had even remembered to give me two duvets instead of one, and with the safety pins that had held my makeshift clothes together. Earlier, I had been able to pin them together and cover myself completely.

It was as if she could see the world through my eyes. Also, the way she had yelled at me for leaving a mess in the bathroom had told me she was someone who judged people by their actions, not their appearance. Silke had never kicked my ass the way I would have needed it, the way that skinny girl had.

Who would live out here by themselves in the middle of nowhere? The bus station close to the Autobahn where I had gotten off was two miles outside the city but Ela had taken us even further into the woods, uphill and onto a smaller, clearly not much-frequented road with bumpy pavement. There had been a single demolished house on the right that seemed to have been a restaurant a decade or so ago, and finally, that invisible little turn-off hid by trees that led to this house.

I would have expected a cabin but despite its small size it was definitely a house, and it didn't contain rough-hewn log furniture but high-end equipment that would have looked more fitting in some metropolitan condo. The layout was perfect for one person, with a small, open kitchen and a rectangular wooden table on the left side, a desk with a computer tucked into the far-left end and the living area to the very right. The front door faced two other doors, the one to the bathroom and the other to the bedroom I hadn't seen yet.

And I would never see it either. She and the reason for her isolation were none of my business and she didn't seem eager to share. I didn't feel like talking anyway, and not just because I was staring into the face of some pretty tough questions I had no answer to. Silke would drive me up the wall with her chatter sometimes, although right now I'd give anything for her prattle. Even if I managed to drop enough weight to convince her I had changed, that would take me at least one year and Silke wasn't the type of girl who stayed on the market for long. And even if she did, hers was no guarantee she'd take me back. If I had let myself go this much once, I could backslide anytime.

Again, I pushed myself onto my back until gravity took over and I staggered onto my right, feeling everything settle into place again. Did anything hang out? No. Good. The sight would be sure feeling to give Ela nightmares. What was I going to say to her in the morning? Probably not much since I'd reassured her and she'd be getting rid of me soon.

I'd ask her to drop me off at the bus station where I'd got off earlier. Thank God I still had enough change left for that. But where would I go? Silke's? I had to pick up my stuff but I couldn't call her and ask for some time to myself until I had packed all. My wallet had been in my back pocket when I'd left her place but I hadn't thought to grab my phone, too, and I didn't know her cell number offhand since she switched plans so often. Suddenly panic ate at me. Where would I go once I had packed?

Friends? Those I shared with Silke was out of the question. I had friends of my own but two of them were couples with little kids who had no space for an elephant like me. One of them was single but lived in a petite two-bedroom apartment. My best and oldest friends, Lars and Evelyn, actually had a spare room but Lars's words still rang in my ears all too clearly: "Blake, you're my oldest friend but you're also the biggest slob on earth. If you ever need a place to crash, I'll be happy to refer you to someone who deserves it." He'd given me a playful punch on the arm after that but he'd meant it none-theless.

Should I call my parents instead? No, no way. Between my mother babysitting me and my dad is on my ass all the time about cleaning up my act, I'd never see a moment of peace, let alone get down to a healthier weight.

A new place? Not an option either. No landlord would take a fat-ass like me who might very likely wreck the shower or toilet and who didn't have a job.

A diet clinic? I'd briefly Googled it a while ago as a favour to Silke but found out that my insurance would only cover parts of it, and without a job, there was no way to afford co-pays.

A cheap motel? Even that would be too expensive in the medium run and left alone, my eating would spin out of control even more.

An abandoned house? Even if I found one, without heat I wouldn't last long in this weather, and I would be all on my own, too. It would be only a matter of time until I either froze or ate myself to death.

Suddenly not only panic ate at me, but I also felt the heat on my cheeks even though nobody was around to hear the soft but high-pitched squeak that would morph into the call of the wild soon. I probably weighed something in the upper 400s, was facing homelessness and all my gut could care about was food. Would that damn thing never stop? Abruptly I noticed that it was the first time I'd felt actual hunger in… how long had it been? Weeks? Months even? I'd been digesting some lasagna when Silke had come in and launched into her yelling fit, and since then all I'd eaten was Ela's broth, which was basically just water. Did I dare check her fridge— no, impossible. She might decide to go to the bathroom that very minute. I shouldn't care since I couldn't possibly make a worse impression on her but I just couldn't let her catch me at her fridge.

At some point even the guilt, the hunger and the despair weren't enough to keep me awake any longer and gradually I drifted off.

CHAPTER FOUR

Ela: Responsibility

Health was vital to my sheltered existence. No doctor or dentist would let me sit through a consultation scarfed and gloved, and even if I asked them to wear rubber gloves, they were bound to brush my skin with their forearms at some point. I knew it was only a matter of time before I seek medical attention but until then I took care to delay the inevitable. I treated my body to sufficient exercise, made sure I kept my environment clean and ate a balanced diet, including sufficient hydration. The latter, however, led to regular nocturnal bathroom visits, this time prodding me out of bed around three in the morning.

As I padded towards the bathroom door, knowing my way around in the dark as well as in broad daylight, my eyes fell over to the hulking figure on the couch. Suddenly yesterday's events came rushing in, shooting adrenaline into the furthest recesses of my body. Blake, the morbidly obese suicide candidate I had picked up from the side of the road yesterday. Again, I felt the slight tingle but while I relieved myself it was mostly concern I felt: what might have happened to him? Not just for him to end up on a bridge with a death wish, but before that: what would cause a person to blow up like this? Whatever it was, I would never know. In a few hours I would drop him off somewhere, probably at the bus station, and each of us would get on with their lives, which was best for everyone involved. I had done my part but could do no more.

Normally I woke up around eight but this morning my stomach reminded me an hour earlier that two bowls of broth presented thoroughly insufficient fare. However, given my one-room layout next door, silencing the snarling beast that inhabited my stomach meant facing Blake. Appealing though putting off the confrontation was, I would have to do it eventually, so I swung my legs over the edge of my twin-size bed and got dressed in jeans as well as a thin burgundy turtleneck and stuffed my thin gloves into my back pocket.

Although I had severely cut down on the stress-induced caffeine consumption of my former life, one mug of coffee with milk was a requirement, and I always relished the smell and taste of the freshly ground Vietnamese coffee beans. A business trip to Vietnam and Cambodia had caused me to switch to this brand for good but had also made an impact on more than my morning drink. For instance, I had also had one of those spray nozzles installed next to the toilet that was common in Vietnam. Most of all, however, it had acquainted me with the local belief system in this part of Asia, in particular, the concept of Karma.

Hoping with all my heart that what I had done for Blake would enter favourably into mine, I pushed the power button of my high-end coffee machine, cringing at the noise of the appliance coming to life. A moment later, a rustle of fabric indicated that my guest was awake. Quickly I slipped on the gloves and kept my back to the living area until I heard my poor couch groan and knew Blake had hefted himself to his feet. At last, the shuffling footsteps stopped behind me.

"Morning."

The voice sounded deeper and gravellier than the night before. Steeling myself for the encounter, I turned, only to find my houseguest at a respectful distance.

"Morning."

Blake was back in his normal clothes, as far as one could call the tent-like jeans, a checkered shirt and blue T-shirt underneath normal. Incredible that clothes existed that fit a man like him, but even these size jeans were struggling to accommodate a belly of that size. There was an imprint on his round face from the duvet, his hair – which I could now see was a light brown with some curl in it – was as unshaven and untrimmed as the night before but he looked rested if a bit insecure. All in all, it was a vast improvement over yesterday, although his size felt just as overpowering. I couldn't help but marvel at how his stature was possible in terms of health and physics. There was also that annoying, inexplicable tingle again but I pushed it away.

"Coffee?"

"Please," he nodded with a grateful expression. "With milk and— uh, just milk if you have it, otherwise black is fine."

His eyes flickered away for a moment. Eager to hide my tingling cheeks as well, I turned towards the coffee machine. "Foam?"

"Uh, sure."

I busied myself with the machine until I felt confident enough I could hand him the mug with a composed face. Just like yesterday, we sipped and stared, facing each other at a 90°-angle. My eyes flickered over to the couch, which was a mess again. Well, soon he would be out of here, leaving me to my orderly existence and relieving me of all responsibility for him.

"Ela?" His soft, hesitant tone brought my gaze to his again. "I- I'm sorry for being such a jerk yesterday. You weren't just being nice, you did more than most people would have done for a stranger. Most would have just called the police. So… thank you again. I still don't get why you did this for me but… I'm grateful."

Blake's unexpected monologue was productive of a protracted silence. Little did he know that I hadn't had a choice in the police matter but hearing him thank me for the rest actually brought a small smile to my cheeks.

"You're welcome." We continued sipping in silence but with considerably less tension. "So, have you decided where you're going after breakfast?"

Blake's eyes widened as if he hadn't expected me to feed him, but only ignoramuses believe obese people have enough fat stores to never go hungry. I used to be one of those but knew better now. Blake seriously needed to cut back but starving oneself never worked in the long run. Now he set down his mug on the countertop with a slight tremble in his pudgy hand.

"Would- would you drop me off at the bus station? The one by the commuter parking lot?"

"Of course." I drained my coffee and put down the mug as well. "Where will you go from there?"

"My ex's apartment to pick up my stuff, I guess."

The answer had come out with a sigh. His wide shoulders slumped, sending ripples through his massive form. His ex? It was the first clue as to how he had ended up on the bridge yesterday.

"And from there? Do you have any friends where you can stay for a while?"

I just couldn't stop myself. Blake stared at me, his face reddening, causing me to lift my palms in apology and step back. The motion caused his eyes to zoom in on my gloves and I hastily hid them behind my back. "Sorry, none of my business. Uh-huh, why don't you remove the bedding and fold the couch again while I make breakfast?"

I turned before he could answer, sensing his hesitation and confusion even with my back to him but waited it out until I heard him retreat. By the time I carried over the tray to the couch table, everything looked neat again, making me strangely proud of him. Silently he then waddled over to the bathroom without making eye contact and squeezed through the door again. Next, I heard the toilet lid clang against the wall tiles. Did he put his full weight on the toilet or sort of hover over it? Or – please no – did he pee standing up? How would he manage that, though, with his gut overhanging—no, don't go there.

When he returned, we shared our meal without speaking, the radio the only source of noise. I turned up the volume when news came on. No mention of Blake.

"I'm not a fugitive if that's what you were keeping an ear out right now."

Busted. Instantly my eyes snapped to his, catching the amused glint in his eyes. "That's good to know."

"Do you live here alone?" he asked after a while.

"Yes."

He only nodded. "And what do you do for a living?"

"I'm an online English tutor." That Chinese service paid surprisingly well and most students were eager to learn. He didn't need to know about my other source of income, my YouTube channel. "What about you?"

Difficult though it was to picture a man like Blake in any occupational environment, it was cruel to assume that morbidly obese people didn't work. A dark look had gripped his heretofore amiable, animated face at my question. "I'm a car mechanic. Well, or at least I used to be."

The reason for the change in tense was obvious. I was staring at it, overflowing the couch cushion and bulging in his tent-like clothes. Was he unemployed then or simply working in a different job now? I had a strong suspicion it was the former. Unemployed, homeless and morbidly obese – what were the chances of him finding an apartment? Zero. If I dropped him off at this bus station and vanished from his life, I was practically sending him out onto the streets.

Again, I shook off the thought. Blake wasn't my responsibility and couldn't possibly stay here until he got back on his feet, and yet the idea was practically yanking at my lapels and screaming me in the face. No, I couldn't. He wasn't safe here and therefore neither was I. I had to stay alone. Decidedly I fixed my mind on my next bite. And the next. Bite after bite until I could almost believe I had left my guilt behind. Not much later I scrubbed away at my poor teeth in order to drown out the sound of my increasingly vociferous conscience.

Blake was waiting by the door when I returned, his hands in his pockets, a posture which forced the mass of his belly even more outwards. It was like staring at a train wreck. Hastily I assigned my boots, coat and other winter accessories to their proper places before I turned to nod at him that I was ready. The words "Got everything?" refused to pass my lips and my eyes were glued to his hips as they brushed the door frame again. Thankfully another circumstance took over my wayward attention: I couldn't believe I had forgotten the supplies in the trailer. Thank goodness the cold had kept everything fresh and no creatures had managed to peel away or gnaw through the tight tarp to enjoy an all-you-can-eat buffet.

"Uh-huh, would you like me to help you unload before we leave?"

A voice that small seemed incongruous with a man of Blake's stature but it matched his face. It was the first time he had offered help and he couldn't have chosen a more welcome time. Storing up for weeks spared me from unnecessary exposure to people and therefore minimized the risk of discovery but it was a monumental chore each time.

"If you really mean that, I would appreciate it a lot."

"Of course, I mean it. It's.... it's the least I can do." His eyes flickered to his sneakered feet again. While I loosened the ratchet straps to lift the tarp, I felt his admiring gaze on me like I always did when a guy watched me perform a 'man's job'. There was nothing admirable about that, though. In fact, despite having become sufficiently skilled at tasks like tree cutting or changing tires, I was not a handy person. The simple fact was that I had to teach myself everything that needed to be done when living in harsh surroundings by oneself, whether I liked it or not, or was good at it or not.

I picked up the first item, a cardboard box full of ultra-pasteurized milk. "Just follow me," I told Blake over my shoulder. Together we stored everything in a separate part of my spacious, well-insulated garage that the previous owner had partitioned off by drywall and that I had almost entirely filled with shelves. Even though Blake had to wonder why a single woman would need enough supplies to feed an army for a month, not a word passed his lips, although that might be due to his lack of breath. With certain success, I tried not to stare too much at the way the load he was carrying was enveloped by his body mass and how his bulges shifted as he bent over to pick up the next box. Meanwhile, he had removed the sweat jacket, unbuttoned the shirt underneath and rolled up its sleeves as far as they would go up to his plump forearms, his flesh wobbling with each bit of motion. Sweat was dripping into his eyes. What may have happened for him to get this big? As self-disgusted as he seemed to himself, it stood to reason that he had brought it on himself and wasn't afflicted by a disease. Why hadn't he had surgery then, before it had spun out of control and before he lost his job?

Hearing him so winded caused the thought to resurface that I thought I had successfully drowned: I had only delayed his death by picking him up yesterday. The way he was going, he wouldn't last long without help. Someone had to keep an eye on him. But how could it work? At his size, we would invariably intrude into each other's space and I couldn't cover myself up all the time. This was my castle, the one place where I could dance around naked if I chose to, which I did on a regular basis.

And even if I adapted to his presence, assuming he wanted to stay as well, how would he pull his weight? (No pun intended, Karma, I swear!) I couldn't afford to cover his expenses like phone or insurance, for instance. Although I enjoyed a steady stream of income, it wasn't impressive by any means and there was no guarantee how long it would continue to trickle. Did he have any means of his own or was there a way he could find work? He needed to stay busy and get healthy.

A gust of cold air brought me up short as I stepped outside again. What was I thinking? I was getting way ahead of myself—oof! An enormous and yet strangely comfortable force bumped into me from behind, knocking me off balance. A grunt, two pairs of flailing arms and a painful yell. The next thing I registered was the moisture creeping through the bottom of my jeans and a heap of panting human dangerously next to me. Instantly I pushed myself to my feet and whirled around to the large man sprawled on the ground.

"Are… are you OK?"

"I guess so."

His eyes downcast, a red-faced Blake shifted onto his knees and heaved himself to his feet with difficulty. Once I would have openly ridiculed him with the finest selection of cruel taunts in my impressive repertoire of derision but now I only wished I could spare him any further embarrassment.

"Are you sure? Nothing twisted or scratched?"

"I don't think so."

Blake grimaced at his left hand and prodded at the row of fresh blisters with visible astonishment. Oh no. His hand must have slipped between my glove and the sleeve of my turtleneck during the fall.

"Let's just finish unloading, OK?" he murmured, at last, still not looking at me, and turned towards the trailer again. We finished the chore intense silence, after which we cleaned and blow-dry our clothes. Despite the mounting tension between us, I couldn't take his eyes off him, milking each second with him for what it was worth. It had been so long since I had exchanged more words with a person than a greeting. His was another human presence in my lonely house in this deserted part of the woods, another pair of eyes beside the ones in the mirror I usually avoided anyway. Still, there was no way he could stay. This had only been the first accident out of many; I should be grateful he had not fallen on top of me. How could I hope to stay away from a doctor's office with the threat of physical harm always looming? He had to leave.

Five minutes later I conveyed us both away from the house, Blake's massive shape cowered on the floor of my van in silence, his body mass again jiggling with every pothole. From time to time he turned his head with difficulty to check on our progress, his eyes shining with something unreadable as we jolted across the bridge. No, please don't consider another attempt—but again, it wasn't my job to take care of him.

At last, we reached the bus station and Blake climbed out of the van. If at all possible, he looked even more desperate and broken than when I had picked him up at the bridge yesterday. Although he was putting on a brave face, all hope had vanished from his eyes that were struggling to maintain contact with mine.

"Ela? I know people say this all the time but... I'm glad I got to meet you. Thanks for everything."

It sounded so final, so fatally final. "Y- you're welcome," I choked out, watching his shoulders slump as if he had been waiting for some signal from me that he was welcome to stay after all. With one last nod, he turned and slowly waddled towards the bus stop. A social outcast, an Untouchable just like me. His condition might not be permanent like mine but if I left him to deal with it himself, he might very likely die. Shouldn't I try to help, no matter the inconvenience or the risk to myself? The sight of his broad back is the last thing I would see of him before reading a small article about a morbidly obese man found frozen to death in some park did it for me.

"Blake, wait." The massive figure stopped but only turned around slowly. I closed the few feet between us with a quick jog. "Do you have a place to stay or not?"

I was looking into the face of a man who had no pride left to lose. An almighty exhale gave way to the answer at last: "No."

"In that case I want you to stay with me until you're back on your feet."

Blake stared at me as though searching for the best entrance through which to crawl into my head and make sense of my offer. "Why would you want that?"

"I have no idea."

"Are you sure?" he inquired, at last, his voice hoarse.

My chin rose with a will of its own. "Yes. Not about the reason but about the fact."

Another deep breath on his part. "For the record, I do have friends, only none where I could stay for longer." He broke eye contact, clearly debating with himself. "I wouldn't take you up on your offer if I saw any other way."

"So, you're staying?"

A little smile broke through, the first real one, revealing his funny teeth again. "Yes, I'm staying."

My own face surprised myself by morphing into a large grin, causing Blake's to widen as well. Why on earth did I feel so elated when the real work had just begun?

CHAPTER FIVE

Blake: Plan

All the way back to the house I puzzled over the mystery in the driver seat. Ela wanted me to stay. Before she had blurted that out, she had looked as if guilt was gnawing at her but once I had said yes, she had smiled as if I'd been the doing her a favour. Why did I let her smile make me feel like more than a charity case? There was no way she could see me as anything else. Silke's words drifted into my mind again: "You need to want to make a change." It all came down to that. Of course, I'd wanted it before, just not badly enough. Did I now? This was my last chance. For whatever reason Ela had decided to take me in, I had to make her see that I was more than a lump of lard and that I didn't intend to stay a lump of lard either.

Ten minutes later we sat on the couch the way we had yesterday, each with a steaming mug of tea again. Just like the day before, I watched her graze her long, thin fingers absent-mindedly over the brown sheepskin she was sitting on.

"Blake?" She looked up at me at last, her face unreadable. "I'll admit I have no idea what I'm doing here. It was a spur-of-the-moment thing, which is new terrain for me. Usually, I plan everything. At any rate, we need to plan right now, and it must start with you telling me what happened to you."

That sounded about as much fun as a sprint but she was right. I owed her the truth, at least everything but the too-fat-to-climb-the-parapet part. Whenever I dared to look at her during my pathetic tale, her pale cheeks coloured a little but when I was finally done, she only nodded and sipped her tea in silence.

"OK, here is how we get started," she began, at last, holding up her index finger, "no 1: pick up your things from your ex. No 2: living arrangements. No 3: rules for cohabitation."

Who on earth used the word 'cohabitation'? And how did she switch from embarrassment to taking charge so quickly? But she was already talking again.

"No 1: the pickup. What are we looking at? Clothes, furniture, car?"

"Mostly clothes, some binders and a few electronics," I answered after a moment. "I paid for part of the furniture and kitchen stuff but I'll have to talk to Silke if she wants to keep them."

"What about your car?"

Just when I thought that focusing on organizational stuff might distract me from the embarrassing situation I was in. "Outgrew it."

This time I didn't dare to look up at Ela again and I didn't need to either. Most likely her cheeks would be glowing like a red light. As casual as she'd been so far about my needs as a morbidly obese guy, whenever I addressed my weight directly, she felt uncomfortable as hell. Honestly, who could blame her?

"A few weeks after I first… didn't fit anymore, the insurance was due, so I decided to deregister it for a while. Since Silke needed the garage and it's illegal to leave an unregistered car parked on the curb, a friend helped me move it into his shed. He owns a plot outside of town. He said I could leave it there for a while, so that's taken care of."

At last, I heard Ela clear her throat and decided it was safe to look up again. When I told her next that I didn't have my phone on me, she suggested contacting Silke on Facebook before she efficiently went over how we would rearrange furniture to accommodate me and my stuff. What struck me, though, was that she didn't look happy about it even though her smile when I'd agreed to stay had looked real. Well, as particular as she was about her space and orderliness, it was probably harder for her to adapt to my being here than she'd imagined. It was tough accommodating another person in a house of this layout, even a normal-sized one who wasn't a slob like me.

She had me put a bunch of moving boxes from the garage into the van – that woman seemed prepared for anything – and we began putting together a list of things she would get at the hardware store while I packed up my stuff at Silke's: curtains for around the couch to have some privacy at night, a sturdy chair, a heavy-duty toilet seat and a shower handlebar for me to grab when I had to bend over. With each item that we added, my face felt as if it was shedding its skin layers. The only bright spot was that I was handy enough to install everything myself, provided she had the tools, which I didn't doubt for a second.

"Ela?" She looked up at me from her pad with a businesslike face. "I want you to know that I really appreciate what you're doing, for whatever reason you're doing it."

She ducked her head and nodded before she got up to empty a chest of drawers next to the couch for my clothes. If women came with a manual, hers would be as thick as an encyclopedia.

Silke finally answered after another ten agonizing minutes. After I had reread her message all of six times, I put Ela's laptop back on the couch table and cradled my head in my now slick palms. That was it then: the past five years of my life reduced to a Facebook message.

"Has Silke answered?"

I didn't raise my head to look at Ela. "Yeah. She wants to keep the furniture and will wire me what I paid for it. I can come over today between 11 and 12 o' clock." After that, I was supposed to leave my key in the mailbox.

"She sounds like a good person."

As tactful and intuitive as Ela had shown herself to be, that was pretty insensitive. Who would say that to a guy who had just been dumped? She was right, though. Silke was not only 'good', but she was also the best thing that had ever happened to me. I had just screwed up royally with her. At that moment I almost wished Ela would place her hand on my shoulder and tell me something trite like 'You'll be fine.' Since I didn't hear her move a muscle, though, my own hand would have to do. As I rubbed my neck and cheek, I felt the scruff under my fingertips, suddenly panicking at the thought of having to face Silke later after all. What if packing up would take longer than I thought and we ran into each other? I looked like hell. I mean, at my current size I couldn't help that but I hadn't gotten a trim or proper shave in months. Again, whenever I thought I couldn't sink any lower in Ela's opinion, reality caught up with me.

"Uh-huh, Ela?" Her face might not look judgmental but it was torture to look at it anyway. "Do you have a shaver I could borrow?"

"Yes. I also have a hair trimmer if you like."

So, she agreed I looked like a bum. "Uh, that would be great news if I knew how to cut my own hair."

A small smile tickled those impossibly red lips. "It's not hard."

"You do it yourself?"

"Yes."

Of course, she did. It seemed there was nothing she couldn't do. "I- I hate to ask you for yet another favour but… couldn't you trim my hair?"

Abruptly the smile was replaced by naked panic. "I- I have no experience with men's hairstyles."

"I think you can hardly make it worse," I chuckled at her, gesturing around myself, which promptly caused Ela to blush again. As tough to read as she was, my size reliably pulled off her mask. Automatically I tried to reach for her hands for reassurance but again she jumped as if I had intended to burn her.

"You don't have to do it, of course," I mumbled, shoving away my wounded pride. I couldn't afford pride right now. "But if you'd like to try your hand on your first male hairdo, I'm all yours."

At last Ela nodded, telling me to shave while she would manufacture a cape out of plastic bags and tape. Soon I sat on her thankfully sturdy ottoman under the makeshift cape while she worked the hair trimmer with calm, even movements. Even though she wore her thin black gloves again, her fingers in my hair and occasionally on my cheeks, temples and neck felt amazing. It had been so long since anyone had touched me so gently.

"Why do always wear gloves?" I just couldn't hold back anymore at some point.

The trimmer stilled for a moment. "Again, because I can."

"Do you want to?"

"What I want is not to talk about it."

Alright, so she insisted on clamping up about the topic. I decided to close my eyes and to concentrate on Ela's hands on me. At last, she pronounced her work finished and handed me a medium-sized mirror. Wow. It looked pretty good actually, not quite symmetrical but an infinite improvement.

"Wow, great job, Ela," I smiled at her in the mirror, running my other hand through my trimmed curls on top and the even shorter hair on the side of my head. I looked human again – human with elephantine qualities. Again, I met Ela's eyes in the mirror, discovering she had been staring at me the entire time, her tense features now relaxing into a smile of her own.

"Thank you. Uh-huh, why don't you wet your hair again to get it into shape? I'll clean up in the meantime, and then I'd say we're good to go."

Once I'd done that, I felt even better about myself. We were running late due to Ela's unexpected beauty treatment but I should still get my packing done in time, and if I didn't, at least Silke would see me showered and groomed. The thought of having to face her suddenly turned my stomach, and I carefully lowered myself onto the toilet. Phew, that had been a close one. Just as I was about to reach for the paper, I suddenly noticed the little nozzle next to the toilet I couldn't believe I hadn't noticed before: a butt shower? A rush of relief flooded through me. First a big walk-in shower and now this handy accessory.

There were plenty of skinny people who believed that big ones didn't take care of themselves, but we do, it's just a lot harder with so much of yourself in the way. I'm not proud to admit I've buried more than one pair of underwear with skid marks at the bottom of our laundry hamper. Silke, who took care of the laundry, never said anything but there was no way she could have missed them. Ela would have given me hell about it but with this little noz-zle, she would never have to. It was almost as if fate had brought us together—yuck, how corny was that? Besides, fate was for people who couldn't own up to their mistakes.

I quickly finished up and half an hour later Ela pulled up in front of my former home where my pathetic climb out of the cargo area was witnessed by a handful of gawking passers-by. Well, when I came back to this area in a few months, I would hopefully do so at the wheel of my own car and in my old clothes. And come back I would. Even if Silke found someone else while I worked on getting my life back on track, I just had to win her back. There was only one like her.

Once I had pulled the boxes out of the trailer and Ela had driven off, I lugged them up to the third floor, pausing every now and then to catch my breath. By the time I let myself into the place I had once called home, my shirt was clinging to me. I really was in terrible shape. Taking in the space Silke had transformed into a tidy home again made me feel… nothing. It was as if this part of my life had been over for more than twenty hours. Only the faint smell of Silke's perfume in our bedroom caused me to gulp and flee from the room instantly. My phone was still charging next to the TV and judging by the few WhatsApp messages, none of my friends knew about our breakup yet. Breaking the news was yet another chore I had to take care of but for now, I had to pack up what remained of my life.

My car keys – useless now – were the second thing I pocketed before I opened the boxes and began dumping my stuff inside, thankfully remembering to pack a few big towels and a huge quilt. I even packed my outgrown clothes. I just had to believe I was capable of turning everything around and losing weight, so the clothes would come with. I couldn't afford to throw out anything that I would have to buy later again. Silke's money, plus my employment benefits and a few savings would tide me over for some time but from now on I had to spend my money wisely.

Packing up my life took longer than I thought. I'd forgotten that some of my stuff was down in the basement, and other things just came with so many memories that I had to hold them for a while before I buried them in a box. This really was goodbye. The sight of Ela's van suddenly pulling up in front of the apartment building brought me up short. She was done already? Had I really taken over an hour? I had to get out of here. Hurriedly I shot off a text to Ela that I would be down in a few minutes and she didn't have to bother helping.

Well, it turned out that it was more than a few minutes and that I could have used her help after all. By the time all the boxes were stacked in the entry and the key in the mailbox, I was drenched and panting again. Thankfully I hadn't met any of my former co-tenants. The building was small and if they didn't know about our breakup already, they would soon. Most likely they would congratulate Silke on finally ridding herself of such a useless sack of lard. Suddenly I heard a key in the lock of the front door. God, please don't let it be nosy Mrs Ackerman—I never knew how reassuring the sight of Mrs Ackerman could be until I caught sight of the person who entered instead: Silke.

Automatically I straightened, running my hand through my freshly trimmed hair as I faced my favourite person with her perfect blonde hair complimenting her beautiful round face with its flawless skin. Her hourglass figure – that admittedly held a lot more sand at the bottom – looked utterly grabbable in those tight black jeans and low-cut sweatshirt and I would have loved to cover her cute nerd glasses in grease spots while I kissed her senseless.

None of that happened, of course, but at least Silke didn't look repulsed. In fact, she seemed pleasantly surprised as her eyes flickered over my face and hair. Maybe she saw I was capable of change after all. Maybe there was still hope.

"Hey."

"Hey."

God, how much I had missed her gentle voice. Yesterday it had been anything but gentle.

"I… I meant to give you the space you asked for," the love of my life began to explain, her cute chubby fingers fidgeting. "I just thought you'd be done by now."

"It took longer than I thought."

"But you're all packed now?"

"Yeah. Your key is in the mailbox."

"Thanks."

Please, my love, I pleaded with her silently, *please tell me to keep it after all.* But Silke's full lips stayed shut even though her eyes were glued to me.

"Uh-huh, you can throw out the easy chair," I managed to get out at last, "I don't think it will live to celebrate another birthday anyway."

"Probably not." The staring continued. "Who are you staying with?"

I hesitated for a moment. "A friend."

Silke only nodded, looking relieved and sad at the same time. "I'm glad. I- I'm sorry it didn't work out."

"Me too." I was still convinced, though, that it would eventually. As corny as it sounded, she was my dream girl. I loved her too much to give up. "May I... may I call you when I've figured things out and... cleaned up my act?"

Something flickered over Silke's face, something that was gone again quickly but that I knew I didn't like. "I- I don't know. I think you should concentrate on yourself and on getting better, and then take it from there."

"Yeah, you're right." But only if that wasn't code for 'Not a chance, you blew it with me.' My gaze dropped to my shoes, then back up at her. "Thanks for... handling this the way you are."

When she answered with another sad smile and glistening eyes, I suddenly understood she had let me go a long time ago. I knew she had loved me once but it was over.

"I wish you good luck." It sounded as sincere as final.

"You too."

Then she rushed past me up the stairs with her head bowed, her familiar heavy footsteps fading away until I heard what used to be our apartment door click shut for the last time, maybe forever. I don't know how much time had passed until I felt composed enough call, Ela.

"I'm coming out now. You can stay in the car; I'll take care of the trailer." If I still had a shred of a chance to prove to Silke that I was worth waiting for, I couldn't let her see that the 'friend' I stayed with was a hot skinny girl.

When the last box was stored, I covered the trailer with a net and slid open the van door. Although I didn't check, I knew there was a good chance Silke would be watching her ex-boyfriend who was too fat to fit into a normal car seat. If I hoped to convince her that I was still worth it, I'd better start working out like a fiend.

CHAPTER SIX
Ela: Rules

When I had caught sight of the big blonde in her thirties with the nerd glasses inserting her key into the front door, I wondered if that was Silke, and Blake's pallor a few minutes later when he emerged from the building with the first box squashed into his belly was confirmation enough. The silence weighed heavily between us on the way back and I couldn't keep myself from repeatedly glancing at the expanse of his squishy back in the rearview mirror. Rock bottom. I'd been there myself and didn't care for another visit, and now I of all people was supposed to help him work his way out? What had I gotten myself into? Helping Blake get healthy in mind and body was already a mammoth project in itself – again, no pun intended, Karma, I swear – doing so while living under one roof with him was quite another.

Forty minutes later my living area was strewn with my hardware-store purchases and Blake's boxes, all of them unlabeled and their contents spilling out of most of them. Although I could make allowances for his wanting to vacate his old apartment as soon as possible and therefore packing in a hurry, I had a feeling this was his default packing technique. The author of said chaos looked around himself with both embarrassment and solemnity before he turned to me:

"Ela? Again, I can't thank you enough for helping me. I just want you to know I'm taking this seriously and I promise I'll try to keep my time here as short as possible. With my track record in diets that isn't saying much, and I can't guarantee I won't have setbacks, but I'll try my hardest. My job, my relationship, hell, my *life* is on the line and I can't screw up. I want to make a change and I'll give it my all. And I don't know how yet but I will think of a way to pay you back."

Just when I had been about to send a reassuring smile his way, his last statement wiped it off my face. It was exactly what I didn't deserve. I had led a useless enough life even before I began to physically hurt people. "Please don't," I shook my head at Blake, "I don't want anything."

For a moment he looked as if he was prepared to argue but then decided against it. "Let's just not talk about it again, OK?"

"OK."

Watching him lower himself gingerly onto the couch and survey his belongings, I recalled the day I had first sat in this very house, surrounded my own possessions. Back then I didn't have anyone, no one to help but no one to witness my struggle either. Which one was worse? It was no use to dwell on the past, though. Things needed to be done. Again, I grabbed my pen and pad and sat down on the short end of the couch.

"Uh-huh, I'm going to make lunch in a while, so before you unpack, we'll need to go over what you like to eat."

His mien darkened. "Are you making fun of me?"

"No." Instantly, however, I felt my cheeks prickle. I hate that about myself. I'm usually in control of my own face but whenever I feel uncomfortable, I turn into a beetroot, and Blake appeared to have a knack for bringing that particular feature of mine into prominence. His pudgy hands gestured around himself while his eyes were doing their best to reduce my lifespan.

"Look at me. Don't you think it's safe to assume I like anything?"

It was like he meant to provoke me to have an excuse to vent or to give me one last opportunity to change my mind about taking in someone like him. Well, not going to happen.

"No," I therefore, responded calmly, holding his challenging gaze. "Or do you?"

"No," he answered after a moment, still wary. "I can't stand raisins, cooked carrots and anything jiggly like Jell-O or runny eggs."

"That's it?"

"Uh, asparagus."

"Isn't that a given?" I mumbled to myself. "Uh-huh, do you cook?"

He shot me an embarrassed grin. "Nothing healthy but yeah. I... I'd like to learn, though."

"OK. Why don't I lead us through the cooking initially and at some point, you try your hand at it?"

"Alright." Now it was his turn to blush, as he did so often. His was one of the most readable faces I had ever seen. "Uh-huh, but I want you to know that you don't have to come up with some diet or exercise plan for me. I need to figure this out myself. You're already doing more than anyone would have."

Actually, I had assumed I would support him in his diet, especially since I had adopted a lifestyle that made healthy eating easy and natural. Although I should feel relieved he was taking that responsibility off my shoulders, it didn't.

"I understand."

"You were going to offer, weren't you?" he asked after a moment.

"Yes. But never mind."

"Hey," he leaned forward with a wry grin, compressing the cushion of his belly, "I didn't say I wouldn't listen to unsolicited advice."

At that moment I realized what was the matter with his teeth: he was missing his smaller incisors. His eye teeth were directly adjacent to the bigger ones. I felt myself smile, both at his words and my own discovery.

"I was just going to say: I wouldn't bother with a gym membership. Integrating natural exercise into your lifestyle is cheaper and healthier. I, for instance, take regular walks. There are no real walking paths around here but as long as you watch where you step, you should be fine just making your way through the trees. Walks will help you clear your head, too, much better than a stuffy gym."

Blake gave a wry chuckle at that. "Aside from the fact that I need to save all the money I can, I probably wouldn't fit onto any workout machines anyway, so if you say that walks might do the trick just as well, that's music to my ears. Thanks."

His gratefulness spared my overtaxed cheeks from heating up any further.

"Any more unsolicited advice?"

"Uh, you do realize that the phrase in combination with your question mark at the end is a contradiction?"

"Absolutely." For someone in danger of taking his own life, he looked remarkably comfortable in his vast skin. His smile widened and his flabby arms folded over his belly, unconsciously pushing it out even more. The sight pulled my eyes like a magnet but I managed to yank them off.

"Well, it all comes down to exercise and healthy eating. If you like, you could just follow my diet. It's nothing special, I just don't eat any sugar and very little meat."

"No sugar?"

"No."

"Are you a diabetic?"

"No."

"Has anyone ever told you that you talk like a guy?"

"No." Because at the time I had started doing that, I no longer had anyone close enough to me to comment on that.

Blake's method of unpacking consisted of dumping the contents of his boxes on the floor and separating it into heaps. With an inward sigh, I helped him repack what would go into the garage, after which he installed the bathroom accessories as well as the curtains around the couch. He also manufactured a chair out of the two wooden blocks and the thick kitchen countertop offcut I had bought. Being a car mechanic, it made sense that he would be handy, and due to his height, he was able to reach the ceiling for the installation of the curtain rails without having to find anything to stand on that would support his weight. Even so, I could tell the simple act of lifting his arms tired him. No wonder he had lost his job.

When the majority of his things was neatly put away, the costs for food and utilities as well as my house rules – clean up after yourself, never give out my address, stay clear of my bedroom and my personal possessions – had been cleared up, we sat down together to rice and veggies with herbal sauce. Finally, we were able to share a meal at a proper table! Blake, however, didn't seem to share the sentiment: just like at breakfast, his downcast eyes and the delicate way he was forking small bites into his mouth made it all too clear he would rather eat in a prison cell than with me.

Clearly, he was ashamed of ingesting anything more substantial than broth in front of me, which meant that I needed to take his mind off our meal, and as it so happened, I knew just which topic would guarantee that. Considering our enforced proximity, he needed to know about it, no matter how much I would have liked to keep it to myself:

"Uh-huh, there is something I haven't mentioned before: from time to time I will ask you to leave the house for a while."

Indeed, this ominous opening caused Blake to abandon his self-deprecating thoughts about public meal consumption at once.

"I… I maintain a YouTube channel and I usually upload once a week, so I can't be undisturbed while I record and video-edit."

His eyes widened. "Are you one of those rare people who actually make real money off of YouTube?"

I only nodded.

"What's your channel about?"

"I'd rather not talk about it."

It had started about one year after I had moved into this house. Despite the regular communication with my online students, I began to feel as if I faded and paled a bit more each day. Most days went by without anyone acknowledging me as a person, and with each silent hour that trickled by I could relate more and more to what it meant to go insane with loneliness. One afternoon, I had just returned from one of my long walks that increasingly failed to re-store me to working order, I caught sight of myself in the mirror in the entry. The oversize hood of my black fleece jacket was still up from the light drizzle outside but with the approaching dusk, the inside of the hood looked completely empty. I looked as invisible as I felt. Remaining fully clothed and gloved, I withdrew my phone on impulse and began to record.

"Have you ever felt like you could disappear from this earth and no one would take notice? They say 'Whenever you feel that way, try missing a couple of car payments' but what if your car is fully paid for? What if there truly is no one who would care? If you have lived alone as long as I have, you have probably been in this place more than once, and if you are watching, that means that so far there has always been something that has made you change your mind and live on.

"So have I, but lately chances are likely that I will come up short soon. In fact, up until a moment ago, this might have been the very day. What changed my mind? This video. I have no idea why I'm recording it or if anyone is going to watch it, but at least it will have served the purpose of keeping me going for one more day. Please don't get me wrong; this isn't a farewell letter, a cry for help or a sick attempt to get attention, clicks or comments. All I'm saying is Karma, you win. I give up. I know you're only a bitch because I was one first."

I uploaded the video without any editing and forgot about it until I happened to click on it again a few days later and discovered that it had received over 11,000 clicks and more comments than I cared to scroll through, e.g.

"OMG, I know exactly what she means! I cried by the time I was done watching!"

"Don't give up, there is so much to live for!"

"What happened to you? Were you in an accident?"

"What do you mean by 'I was a bitch first'?"

There were also quite a few requests for advice. How had I managed to keep going each day? How did I cope with living alone? I had never imagined I could serve as a source for inspiration, and only out of curiosity did I upload another video the next day, again in the black fleece jacket: how to graciously keep unwanted communication to a minimum.

That video received the same attention as the first and the requests kept pouring in. Before I knew it, I told the internet about how to prevent people from invading your personal space, how to keep up your manners when living alone or how to stay fit even if you had no aptitude, interest or financial means for sports. Of course, there were the regular trolls and letches but most of the comments were praise and gratefulness, many of them encouraging me to love myself since I was such an inspiration. I even received thanks from men grateful for my video about gently turning down unsolicited flirting.

Although it pained me to do so, I nipped all of Blake's attempts at prolonged post-lunch conversation in the bud by nudging him to explore the surroundings while it was still bright outside and by setting out myself when he returned. After dinner, I treated myself to a lengthy a shower, wished a bewildered-looking Blake a premature good night and sought refuge in my bedroom with a book. As much as I had initially longed for the presence of another person, the prospect of having my privacy invaded for months to come was more intimidating than I had believed initially. What's more, I just couldn't afford to give away too much of myself or to bond with him. It had been difficult enough getting used to a life of solitude once and I had no desire to go through that again once he left.

All in all, our first few days together passed with as little interaction as was possible for two housemates.

Although Blake had soon resigned himself to my distant and taciturn manner by working on his laptop or spending time outside, living with him was like being constantly injected with adrenaline. Whenever we cooked or ate together, I always had to wear my gloves and make sure he didn't brush my remaining visible skin inadvertently. Even when he wasn't looking at me, I felt as if his eyes were on me constantly, and when he was outside, his presence lingered in the house. It was increasingly undoing me.

On the one hand, I was grateful for what little interaction we shared, which reminded me of what it felt like to be a person instead of a mere digital presence. There were some practical advantages, too: due to the contribution of his voluminous clothes, I finally didn't have to wait three weeks anymore to do laundry.

On the other hand, he disconcerted me. I was never able to look at or hold his tent-like clothing in my hands for too long without my face prickling and my lower body tingling. As unfazed as I sought to conduct myself towards Blake about his size, my subconscious marvelled at and physically commented on it constantly.

All in all, the intensifying tension, coupled with Blake's failing attempts to overcome his messy nature, my nerves were fraying more and more. I could tell he was making an effort but he kept failing the most basic of household tasks: loading the dishwasher inefficiently, leaving his shoes lying in the way or the toilet seat open. I had always been particular about order and granted, these days I bordered on OCD but the fact was that I depended on a clean, orderly environment. I couldn't afford to trip and twist an ankle as a visit to the doctor was simply out of the question. The dishwasher and the toilet-seat issue had nothing to do with that, they simply clashed with my lifestyle and sense of aesthetics.

On the ninth day, I simply couldn't take it anymore. Even though I had asked Blake repeatedly to hang up the damp towel onto which he stepped when he was done showering, he had left it on the floor again in a sodden heap. After I had wrung it out, I marched into the living room where Blake was looking for something in the chaotic interior of the chest of drawers.

"How many times do I have to tell you," I brandished the wet towel in his astonished face as he turned, "fabric gets mouldy! Please pick and hang up your towel once you're done showering! How can a grown man still be incapable of cleaning up after himself?"

"And how can a person your age already be so set in her ways?" he shot back immediately, "seriously, Ela, who gets this upset over a silly towel? If I'd known you have OCD, I'd have thought twice about staying with you! Geez, and I thought I was impossible to live with!"

It was as if he'd punched me in the gut. Calling on every bit of willpower, I straightened, marched back into my bedroom where I draped the towel over the radiator and dressed for a walk. Back in the main area, I slipped into my boots and coat, as always avoiding my reflection in the small mirror. Facing myself was difficult most days, and now even more so. Blake had hit the nail on the head: I was impossible to live with, albeit for a bigger reason than he thought. From the corner of my eye, I saw him take a step towards me but then hesitate. No, there was no way I would facially invite him to apologize. For one, I didn't deserve it, and for another, he had obviously meant every word. A moment later I shut the door behind me.

For the first few minutes that I trudged through the sodden woods, a light layer of snow coating the trees, roots and rocks, my mind couldn't seem to settle on any particular thought. Only after a while did I feel myself grow calmer and my thoughts focused. How much longer could I bear sharing my space with a person as sloppy as Blake? If things continued this way, I would definitely break at some point. The problem was, I couldn't afford to. I practically made a promise to let him stay indefinitely, so he trusted and depended on me. Also, how would a broken promise impact my karma?

And there was something else, something that I was loath to admit to myself but that kept pushing into the foreground of my troubled mind: the thought of a folded, orderly couch, no tent-like clothing in my hamper and the prospect of all-day silence felt like a tightening noose around my throat. Despite his messiness, I didn't want Blake to leave. Oh God, what was I supposed to do?

When I returned to the house after what felt like an hour, the sight of freshly spread and compacted gravel in front of the garage gate and the door brought me up short. I had meant to fill in the potholes soon but current events had driven the thought from my overtaxed mind. A quick peek inside the house revealed that Blake's winter jacket was still there but his boots were missing. Could he be in the garage?

I was greeted by the sight of my van leaning heavily to the right and a pair of thick legs protruding from the passenger side. My sloppy housemate was wedged into the passenger seat rear end first, cleaning the windshield from the inside. The windows already looked sparkling from the outside. There was no way he hadn't heard my footsteps but he seemed bent on playing the ignoring game. Well, he didn't know who he was up against since bearing silences was probably my biggest forte, a skill honed by necessity.

At last a growl emerged from the inside of the van. "You've got to take better care of your car."

"Don't tell me what to do," I shot back, biting back a smile.

"On the contrary," Blake sent a dark look my way, "since you don't seem to know shit about cars." He yanked himself out of the seat and onto his feet, running a shirt sleeve across his glistening brow. "For instance, the next time you get gas, check your tire pressure."

He sounded hostile but I refused to prolong our fight. "I do that," I replied simply.

"Well, do it more often," he snapped, but with less sting to it. "Seriously, you can save yourself some costly car inspections if you check on a few things yourself in regular intervals."

"I'm just not a technical person and YouTube tutorials only get you so far."

"I'm not talking about replacing parts or anything like that. Let me show you something."

He waddled to the front of my van where his thick fingers slipped under the hood that hadn't been closed all the way, opened it and put the prop into place. "Here," he held up the dip stick once he had dipped it inside the oil tank. "See this brown cream-cheese-like stuff?" Ew, gross. "You shift up too soon. From time to time you need to give your engine a workout. I guess you mean to save on gas but don't do it at your engine's expense." He cleaned and put the dipstick back. "Also, have you ever cleaned the inside of your gas cap?"

"Uh-huh, I suppose I haven't. I always drive my car through the car wash when winter is over and I guess I've never thought about it."

"And that from the woman who probably irons her rags," he grumbled but I could tell it was tinged with amusement. "Well, from now on you have to. Every part needs regular cleaning, and considering winter lasts at least four months in this area, you need to clean your car, especially the underbody, more often than once a year. You're such a neat freak with everything else."

"You're right."

Although he looked taken aback at my lack of belligerence, apparently, he couldn't resist poking me further. "And most of your off-brand cleaning crap needs to go. I'll put together a list for you with a few things that will save you space in the garage, last you forever and be much more effective."

I could only stare at Blake in wonder. So, this was the man he used to be: confident and in charge.

"See," he added when I didn't argue, "maybe it was a good idea to take me in after all."

"Maybe," I smiled back, watching him unsuccessfully suppress one of his own. It looked quite endearing, especially with his funny teeth, and the feeling instantly spread throughout my body. "Uh-huh, are you hungry yet?" I asked, feeling my face heat up again and watching his follow suit.

"Yeah."

"I'll make something."

"Uh, I was going to finish up anyway. I'll help you."

"OK."

By the time we sat down at the kitchen table, less than twenty words had been exchanged. We had worked together productively but our fight was still hovering in the room like a malodorous cloud.

"Blake?" He looked up at me with an expectant face. "I'm aware I'm a pathetic recluse with paranoia and OCD but I'm all those things because I don't have a choice. I'd give anything to be normal again." Crap, I hadn't meant to let that last word slip out. Well, perhaps he hadn't noticed. "Nevertheless, I'm sorry. I'll try to work on it and if you try, too, maybe we won't get into each other's way too much."

"You're not pathetic," Blake answered after a moment in a gentle voice, "in fact, I think it's impressive as hell how you're pulling off life by yourself. Yeah, you should lighten up a little bit as you said, if I'll pull myself together, we should get along pretty well."

That night was the first night I didn't feel the need to flee from his presence. We quickly agreed on a movie and I picked up the beginnings of a black scarf I had been crocheting over the past weeks. After a while I noticed Blake's broad fingers fidget like a recent non-smoker in dire need of a cigarette. Could it be sugar cravings?

"Blake, what's wrong?"

"Huh?"

Catching my eyes on his hands, he blushed and stopped. I was probably spot on with my suspicion or he wouldn't be this embarrassed. Should I really add to it by addressing the point? Then again if I didn't, he might break down and raid the fridge later tonight. He probably hadn't so far because I would find out, but any addict was at risk of breaking down sooner or later. My face was ablaze but I had to come out and say it. On the off chance that I was wrong, perhaps he could put my advice to use when the time did come. I paused the movie.

"I'm afraid I don't have any snacks but in case you crave something sweet, a slice of bread with honey usually does the trick." Instantly he flushed crimson and I knew I had hit the jackpot. "Or if it's salt, try lox."

After a few more silent seconds Blake looked as if he was about to pop. At last, he blurted, "How would you know about cravings?" His chubby hands gestured around my torso.

"Never assume anything about people," I quietly told him before I rose and crossed over to the bathroom.

"Ela?" Blake's voice caught up with me just as I reached for the door handle. "If I've said something wrong, I'm sorry."

"It's OK." I even mustered a small smile. I probably spent five entire minutes in the bathroom but that's what it took for me to compose myself.

When I finally reemerged, I caught sight of a sticky knife and the honey jar still sitting on the kitchen counter. Blake greeted me with a tray on his knees and a guilty face.

"Hey. Uh-huh, your honey tip helped, thanks."

"I'm glad."

I could see his face working on the next part. "How do you know this stuff?" he finally blurted. "Did you use to be big?"

"No."

Whatever elaboration he was waiting for; he would wait in vain. I had left my past shallow life with its superficial physical ideals and an accompanying string of diets in the past where they belonged.

"Just one thing," I added, "would you please wash up your stuff right away?"

"I wasn't sure if I was done— "His cheeks flushed and his lips clamped shut.

"Oh, OK then. Uh-huh, want to continue with the movie?"

"Uh, sure."

Just before I pressed 'play' again, I turned to him once again: "Blake? You never have to justify yourself to me for what or how much you eat, OK? I know it's easily said but I mean it."

CHAPTER SEVEN

Blake: Friends

a sdf asdf as as as df df df – how did people learn how to type without dying of boredom? Still, I knew I had to work on my pathetic computer skills. The time it took to get down to a healthy size again would be a huge gap on my resume and I needed have something to show for it. I could ask Ela for help since she seemed to be a computer whiz but my pride just wouldn't let me. It's like I had something to prove to the woman that was good at everything but cars, and hot on top of that. Just looking at her reminded me of what a pathetic failure I'd let myself become and so I practised typing, image editing and ploughed through 'Microsoft Office for Dummies' every day. I actually saw some progress but the fact was that I needed my real job back. Taking care of Ela's poor van that showed all the signs of neglect by the typical ignorant driver had proven that all too clearly. Yeah, it was still difficult to manoeuvre – crouching to check on her tires had been a mean feat – and I didn't have my tools and equipment but I missed my work.

I missed the conversation, too. Just two nights ago I'd thought things were finally looking up between me and Ela. We'd cleared the air and were both making an effort to work on ourselves. I knew she could be funny if she let it out, she was sharp as a whip and full of advice. In a way, she was still a stranger to me but in another, she seemed like only one who knew what I was going through. That honey/lox tip, for instance, was helping immensely. It didn't hurt that she wasn't hard to look at either. But after only three days, Ela had begun to lock herself in her bedroom again immediately after dinner. We had lived together for almost two weeks and still knew nothing about each other. How long had she lived out here by herself? Didn't she ever get lonely or scared? Were there no neighbours? What about her family? And most importantly: what was it with the gloves?

There were so many things she was unwilling to talk about, her YouTube channel for instance, even though I was dying to know what kind of things she shared online that she could earn actual money with. That fact had even made me briefly consider setting up my own channel. Skinny people would be amazed and most likely repulsed by the fat subculture out there but the fact was that there were millions of FAs and FFAs – fat admirers and female fat admirers – out there. Why else would videos of BHM and BBW – big handsome men and big beautiful women – broadcasting naked belly rubs show several ten thousand clicks? Why would the so-called 'gainers' who wanted to get bigger receive PayPal donations to finance their lifestyle? There were even compulsive feeders seeking feeders and stuffing them, sometimes to the point of immobility.

Silke being a part of this world, though, was one of several reasons why setting up my own channel would never work: the odds were too high that she would come across and recognize my body, and watching me flaunt it to the world wouldn't exactly boost her confidence that I was trying to turn my life around. Flaunting was the last thing I felt like doing with my body anyway. But most of all: I would need privacy to record these videos. Ela wasn't away from the house often enough for me to do that, and asking her would entail an explanation I just couldn't give to a skinny girl. She would be even more disgusted than she had to be already. What else would cause her to keep such distance between us? Yet sometimes I thought I saw something more: fear. Of what? Germs? There were some powerful phobias out there but was that it?

Reflexively, I pulled the lid of my laptop shut. It was no use trying to practice typing anymore, my concentration was shot anyway. I had to get out of this house. I needed people who cared about me and who made me feel better instead of worse, and in my current state, even the friendly ribbing from the guys at the garage could very well push me over the edge. No, I couldn't face them like this. Lars and Evelyn, that's who I had to see. I'd texted and told Lars about my breakup on my second day at Ela's and he'd written back I could come by any time since things were quiet in his job at the moment. Well, now I would take him up on his offer. The two of them would be shocked at the sight of me but they wouldn't judge.

It was over half a mile from the closest bus station to Lars and Eve's house, and by the time I finally reached the two-story sandstone building from the 1920s I was sweating and out of breath again. Still, riding on a bus full of gawking people and lugging my huge body on foot beat having to ask Ms Perfect to drive me. Her reminder before I left not to give out her address was enough I needed from her.

Just like I'd imagined, my friends' eyes bulged when they opened the door to me. Actually, I knew I'd lost a bit of weight since my pants felt a little less snug but the last time they had seen me had been fifty or so pounds ago. Of course, it would be months before anyone saw any progress but I'd take every ounce less. Living with Ela might come with a price tag but it worked.

"God, you're huge," Lars shook his head when even his long arms couldn't reach around me for our hug. He is one of those lanky guys that never gain an ounce of weight but at least I wasn't going bald the way he did, and I told him so. Eve, who now wore her curls in a honey-coloured bob, only smiled at me when she stepped forward but her shock at my size was obvious. Hugging a woman as short as Eve proved even more difficult, especially with the addition to a six-month baby belly to her usual curves. As difficult as the logistics had become, though, hugging my friends made me realize how long I'd gone without being touched by another person this way. God, was I overdue.

I almost stepped into their den with my muddy boots on but two weeks of living with Ela were beginning to have an effect. Although Eve would never give me crap about it like Ela, she didn't like it either and I didn't want to add to her chores.

"What would you like to drink?" she offered when I'd followed them into their roomy kitchen with the thankfully sturdy bench around the large scuffed oak table.

"Do you have Diet Coke?" I was becoming fed up with water. Ela didn't even keep juice in the house and lemon slices just didn't cut it. As greedily as I took my first swallow of the fizzing brown liquid, though, all the more would I have liked to spit it out.

"Holy crap, that's sweet."

Lars's eyebrows rose. "It's Diet Coke, what did you expect?"

"Not this." I heaved myself off the bench again, refilled my glass with tap water and gulped it down to get rid of the yucky fake sweetener taste. "I think I'll stick to water after all. It's better for me anyway."

Eve suggested we take it into the living room while she finished up lunch, thankfully a healthy one. Although I craved a pizza like mad, I couldn't afford to slip up in my diet, and after the Diet-Coke experience, I suspected my system might not welcome a pizza the way it used to.

"Out with it, big guy," Lars began once we were sitting on the couch. "You only texted that you and

Silke had broken up and that you were staying with a friend. Should I feel offended you didn't call me the moment it happened?"

It felt as though my laugh was the first one in weeks. "Should you feel offended that I didn't ask you if I could clutter your house with all my stuff, seriously?"

Lars returned my laugh. "Fair enough. Still, I'm sure we could have put up with you for a few weeks."

I shook my head. "I know you'd do anything for me in theory but don't you remember the time I spent two nights here?"

"Do I remember? The stains on the carpet remind me every day."

"See? Besides, I'm looking at months, not weeks."

Lars's face grew serious at that. "And you have a friend who will let you stay with him for that long?"

"Her."

"Her?"

"Not what you think," I waved his rising eyebrows back down, "she has nothing to do with the breakup. I mean, can you imagine anyone jumping this?" I gestured around myself with a bitter grin.

My friend shrugged. "Silke did."

"Not lately."

Lars fell silent and at last, I told him my whole story, with some minor editing: instead of the bridge scene I told him I had called Ela and taken the bus to her place.

"How come you've never mentioned this Ela?" Lars asked when I was finished. "And how do you know her anyway?"

"She brought her van to our garage once and we got to talking. And I've never mentioned her because we haven't been in touch a lot lately."

If interpreted the literal way, it wasn't even a lie. Except for her giving me a haircut and my bumping into her, we had never touched.

"And where does she live? I mean, so I'll know where to come to visit."

"She's a very private person. She doesn't like to hand out her address."

"Why not?"

"It's complicated."

Lars's high forehead rippled and he leaned forward. "Blake, what's going on? I've never heard of this Ela and it sounds like you don't ever want us to meet her either."

"I do, I just don't know if she does."

Lars shook his head. "That doesn't sound like the type of person you'd be friends with."

"People change." That had to do for now; I could hardly explain the truth to him.

"And this Ela will take you in for whatever time you need?"

"That's what she said." A sigh escaped me when I thought back to how she always seemed to flee from me. "I just hope she won't change her mind."

"What's she looks like?"

"Snow-white."

"And which one of the seven dwarfs are you?" Lars grinned at me.

"All seven put together, I guess," I grinned back.

"Well, you can be grumpy, sleepy, definitely dopey—ow!" He rubbed the spot where I'd punched him in the shoulder. "Seriously, Blake, details. Or better: a picture."

"I don't have one. Well, she's almost as tall as me, killer figure, green eyes like a cat and long dark hair shaven on the right side of her head."

"She sounds pretty cool."

"Actually, she's an OCD pain in the ass," I grumbled back.

"Sounds like just what a slob like you needs. Kicking your ass was never Silke's strong suit." Again, his face turned pensive. "You know, not to speak ill of the 'dead', so to say, but in part, Silke's responsible for your problem."

What the crap?

"Come on," Lars went on despite my frown, "she made no secret of the fact that she preferred you bigger. You practically became fat for her."

Instantly I shook my head. "I was fat before we met."

"But not like this. First, she happily let you blow up and then she kicked you out when it got too much. She should have talked to you long before that and offered help."

I wouldn't let him talk badly about the love of my life, best friend or not. "She did offer help; I just didn't take it. Lay off her, will you?"

The rest of the afternoon passed quickly. Those two were just what I had needed to recharge.

"Sure, I can't drive you?" Lars offered when he and Eve had hugged me goodbye.

"I don't think I'd fit into either of your tiny Asian cars," I shook my head with a grimace, "besides, I need all the exercise I can get."

"True," Lars commented with an uncomfortable expression. Apparently, he'd only now realized how serious the matter was. "Still, don't be a stranger. Call or Skype us from time to time, OK? And if there's anything I can do, you have to let me know."

"And you can come over whenever you want, OK?" Eve put in, her eyes twinkling. "I don't know why you've suddenly decided to take off your shoes or help with the cleanup but with this new side of you we might even let you spend a night or two."

While I walked back to the bus station, I texted Ela when I would approximately be home as she'd asked me to do. "Just in case, so I'll know if something might have happened or you're just staying late."

I ended up surprising myself by walking fast enough to catch the earlier bus and also by mastering the walk from the bus station rather well. By the time I let myself into Ela's house I was feeling exhausted but also pretty good about himself, except for the pressure on my bladder.

"Ela," I called to her when I discovered that she was in the bathroom, "I hate to rush you but could you hurry, please?"

"Uh, sure, hang on." I heard the toilet flush and a minute later she came out, red-faced and not looking at me. What was that all about? Just when I was about to dry my hands, I noticed a bit of familiar fabric peeking out from in between the towels under the sink. Wasn't that… a tug not only sent a bunch of towels tumbling to the floor but revealed that it was indeed one of my T-shirts, along with my other pair of jeans. Why were my clothes in the bathroom hidden between the towels? Had Ela— no. No way. Feeling the heat in my face, I yanked open the door.

"Ela?" The face I laid eyes on when she turned was the image of guilt, which only served to stoke up my anger. "What were you doing with my clothes?" Her red lips trembled but no sound came out. "What. Were. You. Doing. With. my Clothes?" Still nothing. "Were you trying them on or something?" Now her pale face flushed crimson, which was answer enough. "Are you freaking kidding me?! What the hell is wrong with you? Did you want to know what it feels like to be a freak show? Why don't you order a fat suit, too? I know what you must think of me but have you ever heard of basic human decency?"

For what felt like a minute, my own heavy breathing was the only sound in the room. Still no explanation from the woman with the glowing face in front of me.

"This isn't working out for either of us," I finally choked out. "I thought so even before… this happened. The more you got on my case about breaking one of your precious rules, the more I wondered why you'd offered to let me stay here in the first place. I'm aware this is your house and that I'm in your space all the time, three times more so than the average person, but I'm trying! And still, I can't seem to do a single thing right!" I closed my eyes for a moment. "I can't live like this. Whatever reason you had for taking me in, obviously you're regretting your decision. It's no wonder you live alone, and you probably always will."

Ela flinched as if I had struck her and her face suddenly did honour to her name but I was done being considerate. "I'll need a day or two to figure out where I'm going but I *am* going. You'll have your precious privacy back in no time."

"Blake, please," Ela finally put in, stepping closer as if to touch me before she pulled back after all. At that moment I truly hated her. "I'm really, really sorry, it's not what you think— "

"I believe it's exactly what I think."

"I can't be among people because I have a condition!" she blurted before I could fully turn away from her. When I faced her again, her face was still as white as snow but her green eyes were fixed on mine bravely. "I- I'm not ready to talk about it but bottom line is that I've been alone for so long that I've forgotten how much I needed someone close by. Yes, I was trying on your clothes but it was only because I was trying to be close to you!"

What the heck?!

"Please don't leave," she added, almost in a whisper.

Just when I thought there was nothing Ela could have said in her defence. "If you want to get to know me," I heard myself answer, "stop locking yourself in your room. Talk to me. Ask me questions. Sit or stand as close to me as you're comfortable with. That's how normal people do it."

"OK."

I don't think I've ever stared at another person and been stared at in return for as long as was currently the case.

"Is… is everything OK between us?" Ela broke the silence at last in a small voice.

"It will be if you let me try on YOUR clothes. I'm kidding," I added when her eyes widened. "Yes, we're OK."

"So… are you staying?" The hopeful smile that started to spread on her face reminded me of the one at the bus station when she had offered to take me in.

"Yes."

"Good."

I swear the noise she made after sounded like a nervous giggle, only I never thought I would ever use the words 'Ela' and 'giggle' in one sentence. She then suggested she make dinner while I could enjoy a shower. Before I disappeared into the bathroom, I turned around to her one last time:

"May I ask you one thing about what happened before we never talk about it again?" Again, her cheeks turned pink but she nodded. "I've been gone all afternoon. Why didn't you try on my clothes way before I came back?"

Her blush deepened. "I… I didn't get the idea until two hours or so after you left and then I spent some more time trying to talk myself out of it. By the time I was ready to cave, I discovered you had texted and figured I still had some time." She grimaced. "You were early, though."

"Thank you," I nodded at her and closed the bathroom door behind me.

Although dinner started out silent as always, this time it was a companionable one.

"Why do you have an American name?"

I looked up in some surprise at the blurted question, only to find Ela's eyes fixed on me as if I was an oracle she had just asked about the meaning of life. "Uh, my mom got it from one of her five hundred or so romance novels. Why?"

"You said I could get to know you by asking you questions."

"True." I looked at her for a moment. "But only if you give me answers about yourself to the same questions."

"Deal. Uh, well, *my* mom is fond of everything French. 'Ela' means 'white' in French." A small smile placed on her red lips. "I guess she knew I'd inherit her skin tone."

"Huh. What does 'snow' mean in French?"

"'Nigga'. Why, because I look like Snow-white?"

My face gave the answer before my mouth had a chance to but Ela didn't seem offended. If anything, she was amused by my question.

"Don't worry, I get that a lot. And that fairy-tale *was* one of my favourites."

Ela as a kid… it was so hard to picture.

"What is it so hard to imagine I used to read fairy-tales like most little girls?"

Of course, my thoughts were spelt out on my face again. "Uh-huh, actually it is. I've never seen anyone so grown up. I mean, I've never even heard you laugh," I blurted, instantly wishing I could take back that last part. Strangely enough, though, it wasn't hurt that I saw on Ela's face but a sly grin.

"Perhaps that's due to present company."

"Oh, really?" I grinned back at her after I had processed her quip, "are you saying I'm no fun?"

"I can't say since I still don't know you. You haven't let me get very far with my question round so far."

"True. What else do you want to know?"

We took it over to the couch where I learned that she had travelled a lot in her old job, an aviation-industry lobbyist, something I couldn't picture at all for the silent, private person next to me, and that travelling used to be one of her greatest hobbies, along with swimming and going to concerts. Although I was glad to discover she was into some of the same bands as Silke and I, her eyes clouded over at 'used to travel'. Whatever her condition was that had caused her to move here, it was obvious she missed her old life. Well, that made two of us. Talking of concerts only reminded me to think of how much I'd screwed up with Silke. Next, Lars's words about her came to mind. I hated that I couldn't let them go.

"Why don't you write to her, asking her to wait for you?" Ela's voice suddenly pierced through my thoughts and I turned to look at her.

"You were thinking of your ex, weren't you?" I only nodded, feeling my throat close up. "From how she handled everything between you and how sad she looked when she entered your apartment building, I'm sure she still cares about you."

I couldn't stand hearing one more word about her and she had no business in Ela's mouth either.

"Please let's not talk about her anymore, OK?"

As hopeful as I'd been about the outcome of this evening, this time it was I who asked her if she minded giving me some space. The fact that she seemed reluctant for once to see less of me did nothing to cheer me up.

The only thing that kept me from taking out my mood on Ela after a night of next to no sleep was to go on a walk directly after breakfast. Even though she tried to sound and look understanding, I could tell I was hurting her but I just had to be alone with my thoughts. I didn't even feel like teasing her about having enough time to try on my clothes this time since I planned to be gone for at least an hour.

I trudged through the woods covered in a light layer of snow faster than most people would have given a guy like me credit for. Blindly I plodded on, not caring where I was going. With the Autobahn as a sort of landmark, it was pretty much impossible to get lost anyway. Only when the sound of my own laboured breathing became louder than the crunching sound of my footsteps and the chafing of my socks, coupled with the stabbing pain in my right side, refused to be ignored any longer did I slow down. When I sank down on the first fallen log I spotted, my fat ass got soaked at once but that was the least of my troubles. God, I was still in terrible shape, no wonder after only two weeks of dieting and regular walks after years of laziness. Silke and I used to love going out for drives but hardly ever took walks together. Lars's annoying words – "She made you fat" – now refused to be driven out any longer.

So far, I had always believed she couldn't have been more perfect for me but listening to my own wheezing and seeing my bulges spread out around myself, I wasn't so sure anymore. Yeah, it had been me taking every bite, not her feeding me, but she should have said something much earlier and made me listen. The more I thought about my friend's words, the deeper they sank in their teeth and at some point, I couldn't take it anymore. All the diet frustration, the helplessness and the self-loathing of the past months poured out in one giant yell that sent birds fluttering and other unseen creatures scurrying away.

When I had no more air to spare, I slumped down on the log again. Who cared if I was within earshot of Ela's house or not? If she had heard me and wanted to know what that had been all about, she'd have to ask. I had invited her to do it and she would have to suck up her shyness. Would she, though? I needed her to. As much as it had touched me to hear she'd tried on my clothes so she could feel close to me, if she didn't start treating me like a person soon and let me get closer to her, I would break.

CHAPTER EIGHT

Ela: Revealed

Poor Blake. I could tell he had slept badly, and despite my good-morning smile and subtle attempts to draw him into a conversation, I could tell that his ex-lingered on his mind. At least he sought recourse in exercise, not food, and I hoped his walk would bring him the answers or the peace he craved. How I wished I could hug the pain away that was etched into his found face. His softness beckoned, he just looked so huggable. Ever since I had watched him clean my van with such dedication, it was as if I saw him with different eyes. His biggest weaknesses, his eating and his messiness, were serious flaws but overall, he was a good guy who deserved to be happy again. Every day he put in an effort to turn his life around and I so wished I could be the friend to help him through it, not just sort of an annoying landlady.

When I had succumbed and stepped into his clothes yesterday, breathing in his scent, I had indeed done it to feel close to him but there had also been another reason: for years I had persuaded myself that this feeling that spread in my anatomy whenever I watched an overweight man was nothing but vicarious embarrassment. It was the only thing that would add a shade of sense to the illogical and unwarranted reactions of my nether regions, wasn't it? Yet with each new day with Blake, there was no escaping the fact that I had never felt the same for large women – in my head perhaps, just not in my body. The fact was that big men fascinated me and apparently always had. Living in such close proximity to a large man had therefore catapulted my curiosity about the veritable extent of Blake's physical dimensions up to a heretofore unknown level.

That wasn't abnormal, was it? After all, wasn't it human nature to explore what aroused one's curiosity and to find out more about it? Right, that was it: scientific interest. Aside from my ability to burn living creatures to a crisp, I was perfectly normal. Yet the memory of getting caught still caused my face to prickle in shame and suddenly I felt grateful for the extended absence of its author.

Huh, speaking of absence, I had the house to myself for at least 45 minutes. Impulsively I did what I had craved for weeks and couldn't believe I hadn't indulged in the day before: I turned up the heat and stripped down to my burgundy satin panties. Just because I had to resign myself to a life without skin-to-skin contact didn't mean I couldn't make the most out of the air, water, a soft sheepskin or smooth fabric caressing my body. Before Blake had stepped into my life, I had always slept nude, too, and I missed the freedom of being able to do all those things.

A few minutes later, I danced and sang along to my favourite band, exploiting the full capacity of my excellent speakers. With no neighbours, hardly any walkers and Blake went, I was free. How much I had missed the sensation of my sheets against my hairless skin! Ever since puberty decided to gift my body with the same abundance of thick black hair I enjoyed, on the top of my head, I had always made sure I was shaven all the time, even in winter. What would a doctor think if I broke something and they had to examine a hairy leg? Gross. Even though doctor's visits and dating were relics of a bygone era for me now and I could hypothetically revert to the hair culture of the eighties, I kept up the habit of shaving in order to maximize the contact between my skin and whatever I felt like rubbing against it.

Suddenly I caught a movement in one of the front windows out of the corner of my eye: Blake! He was watching me open-mouthed, the only thing missing from the image a bag of popcorn. With an almighty yell, I ducked behind the kitchen shelves. What on earth was he doing back so soon?! After I had managed to angle my arm around to the drawers and to tug out a towel, I covered my breasts with it and raced into the bedroom where I scrambled into the first sweater and jeans I got my hands on. When I yanked the door back open to the unbearable temperature of my cranked-up heating system, Blake was standing in the entry with a glowing face, still clothed in his hat and jacket.

"Do you want me to leave?"

"For now or for good?" I threw at him while I marched forward with the mothership of all glowers, which caused him to duck his head even more.

"I'm really sorry."

He painted such a sorry picture that, in spite of my anger, I swallowed my verbal deluge with all its invectives and rash decisions. However, given the rate at which my brain devised unconstitutional forms of punishment, maximizing the distance between myself and the object of my homicidal endeavours was vital.

"I can't look at you right now. I'm going for a walk and I don't want you inside my house while I'm gone. And don't you dare follow me either."

Under my intensifying glare, Blake retreated outside. Once I had jammed my limbs into my coat and winter accessories, I turned down heat and stormed past the large, hunched figure.

My booted feet covered the familiar territory at record speed even though I perceived my surroundings only through a haze of fury. Why had Blake come back so soon? Only thirty minutes had passed instead of the 'at least an hour' he had thrown over his shoulder before he'd left. Was it payback after all for me trying on his clothes even though he said things were OK between us? They certainly weren't now and perhaps there had never been a chance for that either. Having another person in my space almost 24/7, constantly having to watch where I placed my hands and always making sure I was fully covered had long been wearing a hole inside the gossamer fabric that was my inner peace, and now this. I just couldn't go on, no matter how much I needed the good karma and how much Blake made me feel alive. I couldn't look him in the eye anymore. He had to leave.

Does he really, though? one part of my brain put in.

Of course! the offended part insisted. He saw me almost naked, and not by accident either. He knew exactly what he was doing.

But is kicking him out the only solution?

Perhaps not but I just don't trust him anymore. For all, I know he could have been going through my underwear drawer every time I left the house!

At least sleep on it.

That last thought gradually lowered my heart rate out of the humming-bird range. Alright, I would give it until the next morning, provided Blake didn't antagonize me any further.

When I returned, the object of my indignation was slumped on the two front steps. At the squelching sound of my approach, his head lifted and its owner heaved himself to his feet, standing aside to let me unlock the door. I did not look at him while I did so but left the door open in mute invitation. After a moment I heard his heavy footsteps.

"Uh, may I come in?"

"Do you think I leave the door open to heat the woods?" I growled while peeling off my coat and shoes with my back to his wobbly voice before I strode over to the kitchen and began transferring vegetables onto the countertop. Anger had mostly turned to hunger by now although there was still a considerable portion of the former left over. This time I didn't bother with gloves. If he came near me, I swear to God, I might just touch him after all.

"Ela?" I heard his thin voice closer to me after the rustle of his shoe-and-jacket shedding process had ceased.

"Ela," he began anew when I ignored him and chose to wash the peppers instead, "I don't know what else to say besides I'm sorry."

I wished he would stop talking. With each new word he—

"Will you please look at me?"

"No." I sank the blade of my excellent knife into the first red pepper, contemplating to resume the flirt with my earlier schemes for Blake's premature demise. "Whenever I look at you, I'm reminded of what you did. I mean, trying on your clothes was wrong but watching me..." I just couldn't bring myself to finish the sentence; finishing the thought was bad enough.

"What... what can I do to make it go away?"

"I don't know." And what would be the point? He was as good as out of here anyway.

"Please, I'll do anything."

The knife rested for a moment. "I don't think there is anything you can do. I just don't trust you anymore."

"You trusted me before?"

I hated I felt touched by his touchiness. " I did."

His breath hitched, then silence. The cogs in his head were ticking. "What about if you got even?"

That almost made me turn around to him. Instead, I spoke over my shoulder in his general direction. "What do you mean?"

"I… I would strip down to my underwear and you could look at me until you declare us even. That would certainly get rid of the other memory."

What the…

"Of course, nothing short of brain bleach would make *that* image go away."

That mumbled addendum almost made me forgive him on the spot but I forced myself to concentrate on his suggestion. Did I want to see Blake naked? Or more importantly, would it be wise? As hard as it was to cope with my own willful body while seeing him clothed, what would it be like when he was naked? All it would do was confuse me further, whereas what I needed was to reestablish trust or at least some kind of peace between us. Would that make things right again? What had happened to make them wrong in the first place?

"Why were you standing by the window anyway?" the words burst out of me and I turned to him for the first time after the incident. "You said you'd be gone at least for an hour."

His face and body were still at half-mast and his eyes barely on mine. "I was back early because… because I walked too fast. I got sore and too much out of breath to go on." Now his gaze dropped completely. "I never meant to spy on you, I just caught you out of the corner of my eye when I got closer to the house and then… well, hormones took over. I'm a guy, I couldn't stop myself. Again, I'm really sorry."

His explanation and apology rang sincerely and yet my anger refused to subside. Perhaps his eye-for-an-eye suggestion had something going for it after all. "You know what, I'll take your deal."

Blake's gulp was even more noticeable than his subsequent nod. When he turned and lumbered over to the couch, I rinsed my hands and followed him, sitting down in my customary spot on the short end. Now Blake turned. After his thick fingers had undone the buttons, he shrugged out of his shirt, revealing the bulges of his upper arms underneath the black T-shirt that he wore tucked into the elastic waistband of his jeans. Now he reached inside his pants and hefted out more belly mass than I would have thought possible and let it flow unrestrained out of his T-shirt. I had always assumed that he carried a massive underbelly in his pants but now I realized that his stomach had turned so soft and overflowing that no T-shirt was able to contain it, leaving it no other option but to rest in his jeans. Trying on his clothes still hadn't revealed to me the full ramifications of such an anatomy.

All the while Blake kept his eyes firmly on the floor but his face was already splotchy with colour. Next, he pushed his jeans over his wide hips before he carefully sank down on the couch to peel off its legs, his bulges restacking themselves. When he pushed himself to his feet again, I received a full view of bulging calves and Michelin-man-like thighs, part of which was obscured by the hanging mass of his apron belly. Only his bulging hips revealed that he was wearing underwear. His eyes still connected to the floor, the enormous man yanked his T-shirt over his head and began to turn slowly on the spot, revealing a series of rolls underneath his arms, flesh overflowing his underwear and back fat hanging in waves like a curtain on either side of a deeply buried spine. There were creases where I had never thought there could be creases and a rear end that defied the rules of physics.

From wearing Blake's clothes, I already knew how much he had to scan his surroundings continuously, assessing seats for stability and narrow passages for fit, but now I realized how difficult it must be for him to feel his body mass always shift around independently. Whenever he sat or lay down, he had to make sure he wasn't sitting on himself. How many things were denied to him that I was taking for granted? In a way, he was as isolated as me.

Compassion, however, was only a fraction of what I felt at the sight of Blake's exposed body: so much moisture had pooled in my panties that it would be only a matter of seconds before my jeans were soaked as well. Where any sane person would have been horrified by the amount of flesh on one person, all I felt was the need to knead it, to feel how much I could hold in my hands and to experience how heavy that belly was.

Christ, I had been staring at Blake for probably two full minutes. He may have offered to strip but every second that my eyes rested on him must push him deeper into that pit of self-loathing that was practically my secondary residence.

"I'm done. You can get dressed again."

I couldn't look at him when I said those words but I could feel his gaze resting on me.

"Are you sure? I looked at you a lot longer."

"I- I'm sure."

I just couldn't bear it any longer. I bolted, locked the bathroom door behind me and sank down on the toilet, examining the full extent of the damage in my panties. As my head dropped into my hands, it felt almost too heavy with thoughts to rest there. There was only one logical explanation for the state of my underwear and it wasn't vicarious shame, nor scientific fascination: the sight of Blake's naked body had aroused me, as had every single over-weight man I had ever laid eyes on as an adult. They say that in sexuality and relationships every-thing goes and apparently that included being into big people. The notion was more than preposterous and yet deep down I knew it was a fact. I was at-tracted to overweight men.

It felt as if a rush of hysterical giggles was bub-bling its way up my throat and I hastily gulped down some tap water to keep them contained. I, Ela Kirchner, the epitome of opportunism and shallowness, was attracted to a group of people the world perceived as repulsive. Even more ironic, a tiny giggle forced its way out, after all, one of this group's largest representatives shared a home with me and I couldn't touch him!

After I had I wiped my panties and splashed water on my prickling cheeks, I still wasn't ready to face their source. Even though we were certainly even now, how would I ever look him in the eye again? On the other hand, Blake most likely assumed the worst from my reaction and didn't deserve to be left alone with his thoughts one minute longer. He had gone to extreme lengths to make amends, stripping himself not only of his clothes but of his last shreds of dignity. He was serious about giving it his all to start over and to become a better person. I had to get over myself.

When I returned to the living room, Blake was slumped on the couch, back in his clothes. Strangely enough, keeping my eyes on him wasn't hard at all. When I looked at him now, all I wanted for him was to be happy again. Fine, and to sink my fingers into his flesh.

"Thank you."

My two words brought up a pair of eyes filled with incredulity. Another gulp, then just a nod.

"Want to help with dinner? I was thinking salmon and veggies."

Blake's forehead rippled. "Uh… I don't get it. Does that mean we're good now?"

"Not good but better," I replied with a wry smile. "Come on, you need to earn your keep."

A few seconds after I had turned I heard the couch groan and quickly assigned Blake a knife, mushrooms and a cutting board in safe distance from me. When he silently took his place there and began cutting the mushrooms, I noticed his eyes flickering towards my ungloved hands every now and then, and for the first time, I didn't mind it. Anything to prevent his thoughts from straying back to what had just happened between us.

"Blake? Would you be up for playing Jenga after dinner?"

Around, confused face turned to mine. "The block-stacking game? I haven't played that in ages. Uh-huh, yeah sure, why not?"

"Great."

Watching Blake's bloated fingers carefully prod and extract the building blocks while his tongue was trapped between his funny teeth in concentration inflicted even more damage on my underwear. Although I still wasn't close to done processing my earlier discovery, every time I felt the moisture pool between my thighs, I almost welcomed the sensation.

When all hell had broken loose for me, I'd had to leave not only my life behind but also myself as a person. While I felt retrospectively grateful for having my eyes opened to how cruel and shallow I had been, for the past years I had been at a loss to say who I was now. As unexpected as the revelation of my sexual preferences had been, it constituted one major clue as to who I had become.

Plus, not only did my game idea successfully occupy Blake's thoughts, I thoroughly enjoyed playing and getting to know a new side of him. Instead of just a morbidly obese guy down on his luck whose presence posed a continuous threat to my safety I was coming to know him as a person. By the time we were ready for bed, he had knocked over our impressively fragile constructions fewer times than me. I should have known a mechanic would be good with his hands. When we had packed up the game and both got up, I sent Blake what I hoped he would recognize rightfully as my warmest and most open smile yet.

"Blake? I was wrong when I said we weren't good but better. As far as I'm concerned, we ARE good now. Sleep well."

It took Blake a moment to reply. "Uh-huh, you too."

The hesitant smile on his round cheeks followed me to bed that night.

CHAPTER NINE

Blake: Curiosity

A thick layer of snow had fallen overnight and it looked kind of like it had felt between Ela and me yesterday: a fresh start. Something had changed for the better between us, only I still didn't get how. Although I'd kept my eyes on the floor during my strip-tease, I'd felt her eyes glued to my body, and who could blame her? Few people had ever seen such a whale. And then she'd bolted to the bathroom, most likely to throw up. I mean, I hadn't heard her do it but she was the best-mannered person I knew and probably even managed to puke delicately. I had actually considered packing my stuff right there and then but only a few minutes later she'd come back out, looking anything but repulsed. In fact, she'd smiled and thanked me. Actually thanked.

I just couldn't figure her out, and her reaction to seeing me without my clothes on was only one of the mysteries. The biggest one was her phobia of being touched. A skin condition would have made sense but now that I'd seen almost all of her smoking body, I knew she had perfect skin. Was it something that only broke out when she touched another person? I'd never heard of such a thing. Or was it something else entirely? What else could be the reason she always wore gloves and lived in isolation? Could she have been abused or even raped? Whatever it was, it had to be the same reason she avoided looking at her reflection.

The object of my thoughts was still asleep but I was getting hungry, so I decided to greet her with breakfast. I had done so once before but usually, she was up so damn early that I didn't get a chance, and the promising evening yesterday deserved a continuance. I saved the noisiest past, the coffee, for last, in order to let her sleep in for as long as possible, and at last, she emerged from the bedroom, adorably sleepy as I'd never seen her.

"Hey, good morning," I greeted her with a mug of coffee the way she liked it – hopefully.

"Thanks."

Ha, judging by the dreamy look on her face at her first sip I'd gotten it right.

"Wow, you made all this?"

She stared at the feast on the table: boiled eggs, tomato spread, a smoothie and a bowl of grapes and cut-up apples. What I wouldn't have given for some bacon and pancakes, too, but Ela's smile made up for a lot, especially because it looked like she wasn't only happy about the food but about sharing it with me, too.

Indeed, I'd never enjoyed a meal with her more. Don't get me wrong, what happened yesterday was still fresh on my mind, and I bet on hers, too, but things between us had never been better. Ela was unusually chatty and cheerful — not the nervous kind of chatter meant to distract from what we would hopefully never speak of again but the kind that came from a genuinely good mood and pleasant company. She laid eyes on the fattest, most out-of-shape guy ever and turned into Ms Congeniality? She really should come with a manual, and her manual with a manual.

"Could you pass the grapes, please?" I asked her at some point.

"Sure. Watch out!"

Instead of passing them, Ela rolled a bunch of them across the table, sending them all over the place! Quickly I slammed down my arms on the table as a barrier and actually kept most of them from dropping over the edge.

"What did you do that for?"

"Uh-huh, fun?" the crazy person across the table grinned back with all the innocence of a toddler.

"Fun."

"Yes, maybe you've heard of it."

"Seriously, Ela, what's gotten into you?"

"Breakfast?"

I only chuckled and shook my head at that. Whatever was with her this morning, I wouldn't get an explanation out of her right now, and to be honest I didn't need one either. She was coming out of her shell and that was what mattered. After breakfast, we washed up, the washing and I drying as usual when Ela suddenly exclaimed: "Look, dear!"

What the heck? First goofing around and now endearments?

"There, look!" Her bony shoulder nudged mine.

Whatever she'd meant for me to look at, I couldn't care less. She had touched me. She obviously hadn't meant to but she had, and as I stared into the confused face beside mine, its owner suddenly understood and swallowed hard. I was the first to shake myself out of that peculiar trance and to follow her frozen outstretched arm that indicated two deer about thirty feet away. Instantly I felt the heat in my cheeks. Thank God I hadn't replied to her 'Dear' with 'Sweetie' or something. Hastily I refocused my concentration on the two animals traipsing through the trees on their spindly legs.

"Wow. How often do you see those here?"

Again, Ela swallowed and looked relieved at being let off the hook. "Little enough for it to still be special," she answered with a smile, her eyes flickering to mine briefly before they followed the dears' path again. "They are so beautiful."

I agreed, and not just about the dear. The smile currently tickling her lips was the best thing she'd worn since I met her. She wasn't made for isolation, she was made for smiling and making people good about themselves.

"Want to head out when we're done? Snowball fight?" I added with a wink, watching her teeth sink into her lower lip. "What's the matter, think a fat guy can't keep up?"

"No, I just thought it would be pretty unfair, with you being a much larger target."

Immediately her eyes bulged and she opened her mouth, clearly to apologize, but I would have none of it. Her words had been funny, true and from the heart, just like her shoulder nudge. I wanted more of that.

"No argument there," I grinned at her as if nothing had happened, "but I bet you throw like a girl."

It took her a moment to answer. "We'll see about that."

After we had finished up and got dressed, I caught Ela turning her face away from the small mirror above the shoe rack again.

"Why do always avoid looking at your reflection?"

"Not important," she mumbled, zipping up her boots.

"Uh, yeah it is or I wouldn't have asked."

Her eyes only met mine briefly. "What's the point of looking in a mirror? It's not like I have to be somewhere."

"You don't just not look, you turn away." Silence. I shouldn't ruin our promising new start by pestering her but I just couldn't leave it alone. "Don't you like what you see?"

"I don't like *who* I see."

And with that, she turned and led the way out the door. It killed me when she said things like that and when she looked as if she'd never smile again. I would so love to help. I wanted to pull her into my arms and let her have a good cry until she felt better, and then I wanted to tell her jokes until she gasped for breath. I longed for that tiny front-teeth gap to show and her eyes to sparkle.

No, I suddenly reminded myself, blocking out the silent figure in my peripheral vision, that kind of thinking was dangerous. It was OK to feel compassion but not too long for her smile. It would be wrong on so many levels: all conflicting emotions about Silke aside, Ela was just not the right person for me. She was too withdrawn and evidently had no plans to change that. Besides, she was the owner of this house. If things got awkward between us, she might decide I had to move out before I had even remotely come close to my goal weight.

Whatever haunted Ela in the mirror, apparently it chased her through the woods as well, or maybe it was just her default walking speed. At any rate, there was no way I could keep up. Whether it was the noise of my panting or something else, suddenly Ela snapped out of her trance, waited for me to catch up and then matched her stride to mine. I hated how I slowed her down, even if she never gave off a judgmental vibe. In fact, judging by her currently contented face and deep breathing, she seemed to enjoy our slow pace through the crunching snow. She was even walking in relative closeness to me. Once our gloved hands even bumped into one another, which startled her but didn't make her jump. For some reason, she was doing better with proximity when she was bundled up or at least wearing gloves.

As opposed to the last few days, we weren't dealing with icy wind and/or rain today but a mild zero degrees. No sun but no wind either, and coupled with the exercise, we were both getting warm. I had long ago opened my jacket and pocketed my gloves and scarf while Ela carried hers in her right hand in a small bundle. Without her noticing, I stretched out my left hand towards a low-hanging branch to scoop up a handful of snow that almost melted on the spot on my heated skin. Quickly I then stepped behind Ela and stuffed the whole handful into her open collar.

"Argh, what the crap?!"

She whirled around, shaking and wiggling to get the snow out. It was funny as hell. Watching her gather up two handfuls of snow, too, most of all because my ball hit her shoulder before she could shape her first. My last snowball fight had been years and probably more than a hundred pounds ago, so dodging and crouching were a lot harder now, but it helped that Ela did throw like a girl. By the time we were both sinking down on a fallen log, panting and covered in snow, she was laughing harder than I had ever seen her. She looked so beautiful with the small crystals melting on her nose and hair and she practically begged to be hugged. Surely, she realized by now that whatever had happened to make her withdraw would never happen with me.

Ela was on her feet an instant after I'd turned to her and raised my arms, looking every bit the frightened deer in headlights.

"I'm sorry, I… I just can't."

She actually retreated when I lifted myself up and took a step towards her. "Hey, it's OK," I tried to calm her with my palms raised, watching her eyes dart towards and away from mine. "Ela, what's wrong? Do… do you have a skin condition?" Her face shuttered and I pressed on before she might bolt, "because if you do, you should know that air will work wonders. Whatever it may look like, it can't be worse than this."

As always, my reference to my weight caused her to blush violently despite my reassuring grin. I knew I should stay put but just couldn't stop myself. I took another step towards her.

"I can't… I… I'm sorry!" she cried and ran off.

Yes, I still felt for her but at that moment I could have throttled her, too. What did she think I was going to do to her? Besides, what condition could be so bad that she feared I, a guy around 500 pounds, would judge her? She needed me, just as much as I needed her, only she refused to accept help. If this scene was an indicator of what was to follow in the next few months, I already knew I wouldn't last. It had been hard enough to come this far but without any physical support, I wouldn't get much further. Ela's single shoulder nudge had shown me how much I needed someone to acknowledge and treat me as a person, a physical being. I may sound like Eeyore but I really needed a hug. Silke hadn't hugged me in weeks and the way people eyed me like they would a freak at a circus show didn't exactly give me confidence another woman would take her place in the near future either. In a way, I was as untouchable as Ela and it was undoing me.

Whether she had run back to the house or not, I just couldn't go back yet, so I trudged on. Mine was a snail's pace, of course, and I had to take rests, but at least I didn't get sore this time. If I accepted and adjusted to my body's limitations, I could do this. At least one little shining ray on a day that had turned to shit within a few minutes.

In the end, it wasn't my muscles that demanded a return to the house, it was my stomach. I was hungry, hungry for fries, in fact. Great. Ela may have told me to never justify myself for my appetite but she had no clue what she was talking about. At my size, I couldn't afford that attitude.

When I let myself inside the house sometime later, Ela's boots and coat were in their places but she was nowhere to be seen. Only when I'd pulled off my own boots with difficulty and hung up my jacket did she emerge from the bedroom, her eyes not quite on mine.

"Hey."

"Hey." I hadn't meant to answer in a bark but the sight of her suddenly pissed me off. All she had to do was open up a little but no, she had to be a drama queen about it.

"Are you hungry yet?"

"What do you think?"

She glanced up at my tone with a frown but didn't rise to the bait. "Rice, cauliflower and veggie patties?"

"Fine." Dammit, couldn't she snap at me for my tone like a normal person?

Not one word was exchanged during our meal preparation and of course no touch either. Ela always carefully manoeuvred around me and by now I should be used to it but when she actually flinched when I reached over in her direction to open a cupboard, I snapped.

"Geez, Ela, I get that you don't want to be touched but could you stop treating me like a leper? I got enough of that from Silke!"

Instantly her teeth sank into her lower lip. "I'm sorry. I'll try, OK?"

Just when I could have used some of her spirits, she cowered, great. Why couldn't she bark back at me and let us clear the air?

"Weight loss is slow going and that sucks," I now heard her gentle voice on my right, "but I think you're doing great."

"Well, I don't feel great!" I whirled around to her infuriatingly calm face. "Every day is a freaking battle and I've still got nothing to show for it!"

"I disagree. True, you don't look any different but you were keeping up pretty well earlier."

I threw down the knife I'd been using. "You call wheezing while moving at a snail's pace 'pretty well'?"

"Yes."

Her cheeks turned pink but she held my gaze, even when I continued to stare at her. She really meant it.

"Thanks for saying that." Still, her faith in me didn't help much. Resisting the urge of taking the bus to the closest burger place was getting harder every day. "To be honest, I don't know how much longer I can keep it up. I appreciate everything you're doing but at the end of the day I'm in this all alone."

At that moment I couldn't care less how pathetic I sounded. She had no idea what I was going through. Yeah, she had her own shit to deal with but it was nothing a few therapy sessions couldn't fix. After a while, I sensed that Ela was still looking at me and at last I couldn't take it anymore. I had to look up. To call that look in her eyes 'intense' would be the understatement of the year.

"Blake? Will you promise to do as I say?"

"What? When?"

"In a moment."

How can a person stare for so long without saying a word? "OK," I eventually heard myself agree.

"Good. Keep your hands by your sides then."

What the—wow. Ela was standing as close to me as she never had. Now her arms gently settled around my neck and next I felt my soft body mould around her thin one while she pulled herself closer, carefully angled her head and placed it on my left shoulder. She was hugging me! Oh God, how long it had been since Silke had hugged me like that! My arms twitched with the need to hug her back but I had made a promise.

"If you want, you can put your hands on my back, but only there."

I didn't have to be told twice and a second later I felt the hard panes of her back underneath my fingers. Whatever Ela's issues were, she was facing her fears tonight, and her courage couldn't have come at a better time. I hated that I needed her so much but I did. Just by holding me it was as if she was sharing the impossible inner strength she possessed so I could keep going. I wanted more of that.

I'd become used to hugging a short, big woman for years and now I was holding a thin one almost my own height. It was unfamiliar, to say the least, but an unfamiliar I longed to turn into familiar. Softly I breathed her in. Her hair gave off that slightly ripe smell that indicated a wash was due in a day or two but not in a yucky way. This was her scent and the faint smell of her laundry detergent. I could feel her breathing deeply as well. Was she trying to smell me, too? Suddenly I felt her hands run gently across my upper back.

"I think you stand a good shot at a normal, healthy life. Please don't give up."

I literally couldn't speak for a moment. "Thanks."

She might have wanted to pull away long before now but I needed to hold on just a little while longer. These past weeks had taken a toll on me. At last,

I willed myself to pull away before things turned weird and she never offered to hug me again. Yeah, I wanted an 'again'. For once Ela's face was unreadable but her eyes still couldn't be called anything but 'intense'. She definitely didn't look weirded or grossed out.

"Thank you. You have no idea how much I needed that."

Her dark head shook and her eyes turned from intense to sad. "I have every idea. Excuse me." And for the second time in 24 hours, she bolted to the bathroom.

'A normal life'. The word 'normal' seemed to hold more significance for her than for other people. It was as if she was saying: 'YOU stand a good shot even though I don't, and I want you to have it.' She was beating herself up about something, thinking that everyone deserved happiness but her. I had to know what had happened. It was time the gloves came off, figuratively as well as literally.

At first, it looked as if we were back to square one, but a discovery three days later while Ela was out on a walk changed it all: I found her YouTube channel. I still don't know how I got the idea but I suddenly knew that she recorded her videos in English instead of German. My English sucked but there were dictionaries, and I hadn't gotten as good as I was in my job by being a quitter. After more search terms than I could count, I finally hit the jackpot: a user named The Untouchable. The description of the channel read:

If you're looking for tips on how to find Mr Right, keep searching. I try to offer advice to those who have realized that not every Jill has their Jack.

Yep, I had her. When I started the first video she had uploaded two years ago – "Karma, you win" – I was greeted by a faceless female figure in a black jacket. The woman's voice sounded deeper and her tone was totally different but I knew this was Ela. Quickly I moved from the couch to the kitchen table so the screen would be facing the inside of the room instead of the windows in case she came back from her walk within the next few minutes.

I watched all her videos, some of them several times since I often couldn't understand everything despite the closed captions. I watched everything she had ever uploaded, such as "How to do basic repairs and maintenance, parts 1-6", "How to avoid doctor's visits" or "How to keep up your manners when living alone". With every video, one more piece of the puzzle that was Ela fell into place, and by the time she came back from her walk, I couldn't look her in the eye anymore. The video binging this afternoon had been so much to take in that I needed some time to process it all.

An hour and a half later I returned from my own walk with resolve: I would get some answers tonight. During our dinner preparations, I eased into the topic by mentioning I was making progress with my typing practice before I questioned Ela about her impressive computer skills. I needed her to feel comfortable and relaxed so she wouldn't realize until too late that she was cornered.

"You know," I told her causally after we had slid our vegetarian casserole into the oven, "I get why some people choose to go off the grid but you… you've gone ON the grid."

Instantly Ela's face shuttered and she began to turn away. I should have known she wouldn't be lulled into a sense of security so easily. Well, brute force it was then. I reached out to touch her shoulder, causing her to whirl around with wide-open eyes before my fingers could make contact.

"Come on, out with it. You're a digital native but an analogue stranger. Why? You like people. You have good manners, you help where you're needed and you work as a tutor. Why is social media OK but real social contacts are not?"

Her ungloved hands balled into fists. "Stop pestering me about it."

"Nope," I shook my head and stepped closer, which made her back up instantly. "We're housemates and will be for many weeks to come. We've done a pretty good job so far staying out of each other's way but it's time that stops. I want to get to know you."

Now was her chance to counter with 'But I don't want to get to know you' but she didn't, nor did her face. "Don't you want to get to know me?" I challenged her, both with words and my body.

"I…" she swallowed as I drew closer, slowly backing up until her back hit the wall.

"I would never hurt you, I hope you know that."

"Blake," she rasped, "please don't come any closer."

"And why not, hmm?"

She swallowed again, her eyes darting left and right, looking for an escape. It was now or never. I'm a fat guy but I can move pretty quickly in one spot. Before she realized what was happening, I had captured both of her wrists in my hands.

"Nooooooo!"

I felt her pull back but neither I nor the wall behind her was budging. She was panting heavily, doubled over as far as she could with my body in the way. Then I felt her go still. Slowly, vertebrae by vertebrae, she straightened. Her hands stopped fighting and her fingertips brushed gently against her fleshy handcuffs. Now they prodded, gently at first but getting more insistent. The sensation was so eerie I loosened my grip on her, only to feel her hands gripping mine now. She turned my left-hand palm up and pried open my fingers slowly, twitching away from time to time but always returning. Now she prodded the inside of my palm with her index finger while her wide-open eyes kept darting between my hand and my face as if waiting for a reaction.

At last, she looked at me fully, her breath ragged. The new sensation of her standing in belly-touching distance and her skin on mine suddenly freaked me out and I moved to pull back but she held on.

"I… I don't understand."

"No, I don't understand," I choked out after a massive gulp. "What are you doing?"

"Touching you. I'm actually touching you," she breathed.

"Duh, I can see that. Why?"

"Because I can't believe I can."

"Ela, you're not making any sense. Of course, you can, you've just gone to great lengths to make sure it doesn't happen." I hated the sulkiness in my voice but I couldn't help it.

"I… I had a reason for that." Her eyes began to shine and my hands slid out of her grasp.

"Ela, what is it? What's the reason?"

No answer. Reflexively I reached for her hands again, making her gasp and pull away before she tentatively stretched them out after all. Again, she looked at our joined hands as she would at some alien.

"Please tell me," I murmured to her, "I can tell it's tearing you apart. Even if I can't help, maybe sharing will make you feel better."

Several deep breaths on her part. "A- alright."

CHAPTER TEN

Ela: Immune

My hands were shaking so hard that I poured more water over them instead of into the electric kettle. At some point, Blake gently nudged me aside and took care of the tea I had to make do with since I didn't keep any alcohol in the house. I really could have used some liquor right now in order to process what was happening: I could touch Blake. I hadn't been able to when he first arrived but now I could.

A warm hand on my shoulder almost caused me to reflexively jab my elbow into its owner's expansive midriff but he gently slid his hand down my arm and into my own hand, leading me over to the couch where he sat me down in the crook at a 90°-angle from him, never breaking manual contact. This was all too much to take in. Why was the only effect of my touch a thoroughly bewildered round face instead of yelling and blisters? When said face stayed turned to mine and aforementioned hands continued their caress, I finally drew up my legs and scooted closer to Blake. Whatever was happening here and however long it would last, I would avail myself of it. I needed all the strength I could get from him to tell the secret that was no longer mine to keep.

"I'm from Frankfurt, originally. It all started when… when I visited a pet shop there with my friend Denise three years ago to help her pick out a budgie."

I still recalled the salesman in his early twenties with his gloriously rotund body, double-chinned face and a timid smile that caused Denise to pull in a grimace at once as he waddled towards us, only I, of course, omitted his physical description to Blake. The salesman then coaxed one of the adorable birds out of its cage and let it hop from his chubby fingers onto Denise's thin, manicured ones from where she nudged it into my hands eventually. That's when it happened. Again, I swallowed as a wave of nausea crashed down on me. I would never be able to erase the sound, sight and smell from my memory for as long as I lived.

"Suddenly the little bird started to smoke and screech. I hope to God you'll never have to hear an animal in such pain." Blake's warm hands administering a gentle squeeze barely made an impact through the horrific memory. "The… the sales guy started yelling at me what I had done, and after a moment I yelled right back at him, telling him to check his security footage if he actually believed I would hurt an innocent bird."

I had certainly been cruel enough at the time to hurt innocent human beings, at least verbally, but I had also been a master at turning the tables and reassigning blame. To this day I remember verbatim what I had shouted at him while I backed him against the counter.

"Seriously, what kind of birds are these? Terrorist birds? What if I'd burned myself? You're lucky this isn't the States or I would sue your pants off!"

Denise and I left the shop after, both still shaken to the core.

"Seriously," she pulled me onto a bench in the inner-city pedestrian area insufficient distance to the pet shop, "what happened with that poor bird?"

"Spontaneous avian combustion? I don't know! I'm just as freaked as you are!"

Immediately Denise's arm went around me, at least as much as was possible for a 5'2" person's short limbs.

"Maybe it was some kind of disease. You poor thing, you're totally right, you could have burned yourself." Then she snickered. "How lucky you can't literally sue the guy's pants off. Nobody would want to see that."

"Ugh, I agree. Nobody." Although my dramatic shudder entertained and distracted my friend sufficiently, I never succeeded in regulating my facial blood circulation where large men were concerned. "Stupid fat-ass, thinking I'd harm a poor bird," I added for effect, infusing my words with all the fear and shock from the experience lest Denise detect the truth. Of course, I didn't tell Blake that last part either.

After that, it came on gradually. I was still able to touch my friend, for instance, and over the course of the next few days, I actually managed to put the budgie incident behind me. Well, and then came the weekend when my mom asked me to watch her rabbit Hugo while she went on a two-week vacation. The little guy was positively ancient and could hardly move anymore. My mom would often hold him while he slept in her lap, and so on that Friday evening I did, too. I was treating myself to a night in, binge-watching TV shows on the couch. I still remember how fuzzy Hugo was. Well, until I dozed off into my signature deep sleep.

"Like I said," I told Blake, who was listening intently, "the little guy could hardly move anymore, and since rabbits can't scream, I remained oblivious to the torture he was going through until I woke up to the smell of smoke. I… I will never forget that charred lump in my hands. Immediately I threw it off me, called the friend that lived closest and asked if I could spend the night."

Conjuring up a pretext for my request as well as feigning a slight cold when I arrived so nobody would touch me came easily to the professional manipulator I was. My friend Luciana automatically retreated when she picked up on the word 'cold'.

"Don't worry, we're not keen on Emmy catching yet another bug. Besides, she has a ballet performance on Sunday she can't miss. We'll put you up in her room and keep her in our bed tonight and make sure she won't come near you."

Needless to say, however, the five-year-old kid was less than keen on someone other than her occupying her room, and in the morning, she managed to wiggle out of bed so carefully that her parents never noticed a thing. I didn't wake either until

I heard the sound of screaming. By the time I realized where I was, my friends had arrived by my bedside where the poor little dear was holding a pair of blistered hands in front of her, screaming her head off. Since they couldn't get a word out of her nor an explanation out of me, I simply urged them to get her to the hospital while I would show myself out. Later that day, they tried to reach me on my phone but I just couldn't talk to her. Eventually, Luciana sent me a text, demanding I call her since Emmy had told them she had burned herself on my skin.

"Well, I had definitely ruined her ballet performance," I concluded that the incident had kicked off my flight into isolation. Blake's hold on my hands tightened but I just couldn't face him. Most likely he was already devising a plan how he could best extricate himself from this situation and escape the lunatic's lair.

"When I came back to my apartment, I buried Hugo and started packing since I knew Luciana would seek me out if I continued to ignore her calls and texts. Not only did I have no explanation to offer to her, if she noticed I wouldn't touch her, but she would also know her daughter had told the truth. I had to leave, so I contacted a realtor about selling my condo and fining me an isolated but full-equipped little house anywhere in Germany."

"Uh-huh," Blake cleared his throat, "I get that you were spooked but wasn't that a little drastic? I mean, all those things could have been freak accidents."

Not even a tiny bit of regret bothered to make an appearance, so many times had I been over the events since then. "At first I talked myself into that, too, but deep down I suppose I knew it was me. I had to get away."

"And where did you go?"

"A cheap motel about twenty miles away. From there I emailed my mom, telling her Hugo had died in its sleep and that I had given him a proper burial. I also told her I had to leave town and that I would be in touch later to explain everything. After that, I wrote notice letters to my company, my phone carrier and anything else that tied me to Frankfurt. While I was holed up in that motel, I also tested my theory, at first on a half-dead fly crawling on my window sill. At best, nothing would happen, and at worst I would put it out of its misery. Well, it burnt to a crisp within a second. When I went out for food, I tested it on people, too. Just a finger graze here and there but when everyone yelped in pain without fail, I finally believed it."

Clearly, that made one of me. "Hey," I rolled my eyes at my sceptical audience, "do you really think I would have given up my life for years of solitary confinement if I didn't know for sure? Believe me, I have thoroughly tested it."

At last, I heard Blake draw a deep breath. "I want to believe you but… you've got to admit; it sounds pretty far-fetched." The ensuing sharp gasp instantly raised my eyes to his. "Hang on, were *you* responsible for the strange blisters I got when we bumped into each other and fell while unloading your trailer?"

"You believe me now, don't you?"

"Yeah." Silence. "So, what do you think this is? A curse?"

"Most likely it's karma."

Blake's forehead rippled. "You believe in karma?"

"I didn't use to. During a business trip to Vietnam and Cambodia I learned some about it but at the time I simply put it off as part of the Asian culture. When this… thing set in, though, I thought back and suddenly it made a lot of sense."

"How can that make sense?" Blake blurted, at last, his eyebrows contracting.

Meeting his eye had never come easier. The pretence was over. "I wasn't a good person, Blake. In fact, I was a shallow, self-centered opportunist. I used others," I emphasized when belief still hadn't descended upon Blake, "My friends and I would also ridicule people in public we thought beneath us, never bothering if they overheard us." And still, the man in front refused to see the real me. "It's the truth."

His curly head shook with emphasis. "That still doesn't explain why you of all people would have to pay this way. I mean, there are so many shallow people out there."

"I have no explanation for that either. I can only hope to find ways to make up for what I did and perhaps one day make it go away. It's tough to find opportunities for that, though, when you can't be among people."

Blake's face was practically alive novel, narrating every sensation and emotion my tale had triggered. At last, his eyes widened and he scooted away a little, causing his hands to abandon mine and his soft flesh to quiver. "Hang on, is that why you picked me up at the bridge? To get some good karma?"

"No!" I blurted, desperate to hold his hands again but even more so for him to believe me, "when I saw you lying on the ground, I saw someone who needed help, and who needed it fast. Well, actually," I realized, more to myself than to him, "I saw myself. After two weeks of isolation in the motel, I was ready to disappear from the world. I even bought liquor and sleeping pills. Burning myself to death would have been more appropriate but… I was too much of a coward to do it," I finished softly, fixing my gaze on the hands in my lap. "Well, as it turned out, I was even too much of a coward to take the pills."

Although I could have wished for Blake to pull me close and tell me how glad he was I hadn't acted on my death wish, I only felt so in theory. Most days I wasn't sure about my purpose in life, not even after I had invited him to stay with me.

"And nobody came looking for you?" Blake inquired, at last, still not edging closer. "Not your family, or your… your boyfriend?" That last part sounded choked and when I looked up, I found he was wearing the face to match.

"Nobody would have known where to look because I changed my cell number and let a moving company and the realtor handle everything."

"And you haven't been in contact with anyone since then?" he pressed on.

"I'm an only child and have only had my mom left. I... sent her a postcard on her birthday and on Christmas to let her know I'm OK but she doesn't know where I am."

"That's terrible."

"No, I always choose very nice cards."

"You know what I mean!"

I shook my head. "Except for the postcards I'm not in contact with anyone. I would so love to at least hear my mom's voice again on the phone but... there is no way I could explain. Even if she believed me, she would be scared of me. I... couldn't bear that." Again, my gaze dropped to my hands.

Suddenly the couch dipped and a pair of pudgy hands appeared in my range of vision. I could have cried at the warm, soothing sensation around my clammy fingers. "And what about your... your boyfriend? I mean, were you in a relationship when all hell broke loose for you?"

"Thankfully not, which made it a lot easier, not that there would have been much to leave behind in regret. I've never been good at relationships. I drove them all away at some point." Too much work, too much me.

"You, uh-huh…" Blake cleared his throat, "you said that karma wasn't the reason you took me in, but is it the reason you wanted me to stay?"

"A part of it," I told him honestly. He deserved nothing but the truth. "The other part was that… one half-day with you had already shown me how much I needed another person close by and I wasn't ready to give that up yet. Plus," I offered him a weak smile, "over time I began to like you."

His already soft face softened even more at my admission and his hands resumed their gentle caress that I had all but given up on ever feeling again. "So… why can I of all people touch you? Because you got some good karma by helping the best representative for people you think beneath you?"

"I don't think you're beneath me!" His last comment had been added in a teasing tone but this was no laughing matter. This time it was I who withdrew her hands from his. "How could I, an Untouchable in the truest sense of the word, think anybody beneath me anymore?" My hands tore through my hair as though with a will of their own. "And I don't know why you can touch me; I have no idea how this whole thing works! If I did, I would have figured out a solution a long time ago!"

"I'm sorry." For a while, we sat in silence. "It all makes sense now. Wow." Blake, too, ran a hand through his hair before he looked back at me. "I can't imagine how you've pulled it off so far. For instance, how did you support yourself in the beginning, before you became a YouTube star?"

"I inherited some money from my dad and my tutoring job pays surprisingly well. Plus, my living expenses are not exactly high."

Although he nodded, I could tell he was about to burst with curiosity. "I have so many questions, I have no idea which one to ask first," he blurted indeed a moment later. "For instance, how do you go to the doctor or dentist?"

"I don't," I shrugged with a grimace, "hence the OCD. I have to keep everything tidy and clean so I won't get an infection or trip over something and break a bone."

"Oh." It was as if he was taking inventory of all the items he had ever discarded haphazardly, or the number of times he had left the table or kitchen counter unwiped. "And how do you go on vacation?"

Not a subject I liked to dwell on. "I don't, at least not anymore. My last one was two years ago and I don't think there will be another one any time soon."

"Where did you go?

"Oman."

"Oman? I don't know anyone who's been there. Don't they forbid women to drive?"

"That's Saudi-Arabia, and even that has been changed. No, Oman is actually a pretty open-minded country despite their traditional culture."

"But didn't you have to wear a... what's it called?" Blake's thick hands groped around in midair as if hoping to catch the elusive term, "one of those veils?"

"Hijab?"

"No idea. Anyway, didn't you have to—oh."

"No," I put in with a slight shake of my head as realization dawned on him, "it isn't required for tourists but you can guess how glad I was to wear it. What also worked in my favour is the fact that touching, e.g. shaking hands with the other gender if they aren't married isn't customary in Oman. It was pretty warm at times under the hijab but with the right fabric, it was fine. In fact, I haven't felt as free and normal in years."

Despite the precious memory I failed to suppress a shiver as I recalled the flight. "Free and normal," I added half to myself, half to Blake, "were not how I felt during my journey there and back, though. The security check and the flight were hell. All the time I feared I would hurt someone, worst of all security staff. One wrong move and I could have ended up in jail or worse. Despite the wonderful vacation, I decided it wasn't worth the agony of travelling."

"I can't imagine what that must have felt like." Again I felt my hand being enveloped by warm, pliant flesh. "Obviously I haven't been on an aeroplane in years. Silke was afraid of flying anyway, so it didn't matter but..."

"But you miss it."

"Yeah." After a moment Blake shook his head as if to rid himself of the painful thought. "Too bad you're not a Muslim," he looked back at me with a wry grin. "A hijab would be ideal for you in the summer here. It must be a veritable slalom race at a supermarket for you with all those people in short clothes."

"Actually," I felt a grin of my own creep into my face, "I sometimes do dress like a Muslim in the summer when I have to go into town. On other days I go as a goth, with long lace gloves. Dark makeup keeps people at a distance almost as much as a hijab."

I then answered more of Blake's questions until the last word had faded and only the soothing caress of his hands remained.

"Blake?" I spoke at last, "may I touch more of you, please?"

"Wh- what do you mean?"

"You have no idea what it is like not to be able to touch anyone, not even an animal. Please, I would really like to touch as much of your skin as you're comfortable with."

Although 'comfortable' was the last adjective attributable to the man beside me right now, after a telltale gulp he finally nodded. "Alright."

CHAPTER ELEVEN

Blake: Exploring

The urgency in Ela's voice made me hold out my hands to her at once. Swiftly she moved the ottoman in front of me, her knees connecting with my hanging gut, and carefully prodded the centre of my palms again before placing her hands inside mine. Slowly she began to run them over mine and up my forearms, closing her eyes and breathing in deeply.

"You feel incredible."

Yeah right. Only someone deprived of human skin contact would say that. I do have great skin but there's oceans of it. Out of all people immune to her condition, it was me? She was forced to touch the most repulsive body she had ever laid eyes on? Her face told a different story, though, and it was what took away any remaining doubts I still had about her revelation. The whole thing still sounded ludicrous but the more she'd told me; the more puzzle pieces had fallen into place. No wonder she was almost desperate to upload new YouTube Videos in order to reach out to people, why she always caressed that sheepskin or why she had danced around in her underwear. God, I couldn't even imagine what life must be like for her.

Ela now ran her palms over mine and the back of my hands again, laced our fingers, squeezed and exhaled sharply. Then she glided up the insides of my forearms, breathing as if in heat. Her eyes rolled into the back of her head as she practically gorged herself. *On me.* If a fat gut is good for one thing, it's hiding how turned on its owner is, and boy was I close to explosion.

"May I… try if I can touch you with something other than my hands?"

I could only nod, watching her bring my hands up to her face before she carefully brushed her nose and then her cheeks against my palms until I was completely cupping her face. Again, her head angled and her nose grazed my palms before I felt her lips brush against them next. Now I felt and saw her press a kiss down on my skin. Again. And again! Picking up speed, she kissed her way out of my cupped hands and up my forearms until tears gathered in the corners of her eyes and rolled down her cheeks. Instantly I cupped her face in my hands again and brushed away the drops with my thumbs.

"Ela, what's wrong?"

"Nothing," she chuckled, "for once, nothing is wrong with me!"

And then she threw her head back and laughed as freely as I had never seen her. I could only watch the woman in wonder, who suddenly scrambled onto my lap and threw her arms around me.

"Thank you," she breathed into my ear, wet tears against my cheek. Automatically, my arms pulled her close. For her, it may have been years and for me only months without being touched with appreciation but at that moment, I could have cried just like her. Of course, she only behaved like that because I was the only one immune to her curse, but holding her against me felt so infinitely good.

At last Ela pulled back but kept her hands in mine, her thumbs gently tracing my skin. "I could monopolize your skin for hours on end. I won't, though, don't worry."

Damn. I knew I shouldn't feel so disappointed when she withdrew her hands at last, but the fact was that not only did she need my touch, but I also needed hers, too. It didn't help that she looked as reluctant to pull back as I felt.

"May… may I keep touching you in regular intervals, though?" she pleaded, "I don't know how long this is going to last."

"Not- "I had to clear my throat to get out the rest of the sentence, "not a problem. Uh, you don't have to stop right now either."

That last part had slipped out but I couldn't muster an ounce of regret. Reflexively, I offered my hands to her palms-up and waited until Ela placed hers inside again and resumed her stroking. Instantly her face brightened.

"I like it when you smile."

"Ditto." Her eyes dropped to my mouth. "You have funny teeth."

"The better to amuse you with, my dear," I grinned at her, in that moment absurdly grateful I'd been born without my smaller incisors.

After a while, Ela began to subtly rotate her shoulders. Of course, this posture couldn't possibly be comfortable. "Hey," I suggested, "how about we get comfier? You could down next to me and we can go from there."

As soon as she had done so, she grabbed my hands again, almost as desperate as a junkie. "Sorry," she grimaced at me, "you've got to tell me when you want me to back off and give you your space."

"Don't worry, I'm not there yet." Dammit, I shouldn't let her relieved smile give me hope but I pushed the thought away. "Would you like it if I— "put my arm around you, I was about to say, only to realize it wouldn't work. Even if my gut didn't take up so much space that I had to sit with my thighs spread wide apart, my ass and hips bulged over so much that she couldn't sit close enough for me to put my arm around her without leaning to the left at an awkward angle and possibly crushing her. Instantly I felt my cheeks tingle. "Never mind. Uh-huh, what would *you* like?"

It took her longer to answer than I would have thought. Oh God, what if this was too much closeness for her after all? What if her revulsion outdid her skin-contact deficit?

"Were you going to suggest touching *me*?"

No, but that sounded like the best thing I'd heard in months.

"Because I would like that very much. Uh-huh, if it's OK for you," she added, the colour in her cheeks heightening.

"Of course it's OK." If only she knew. "What did you have in mind?"

"Would you touch my arms and neck? I could sit on the ottoman with my back to you."

Hell yeah! Only if I scooted close enough to touch her, my gut would be between us. "Uh-huh, you'll feel more of me than you might feel comfortable with, though. I… can't help it."

She blushed at me, shaking her head. "I'll tell you if that's the case but I'm pretty sure it won't be. I want this too much."

"Alright. Uh-huh, do you have a stool you can sit on instead of the ottoman?" I couldn't spread my legs that much.

She only nodded and got up. She really wanted to go through with this then? She actually wanted my hands on her? Suddenly it felt as if she'd fed ten logs into an oven at once. My shirt needed to go. I scooted forward, silently cursing at how everything swayed and jiggled, worked my way out of my shirt with some difficulty and checked that everything was covered before I heard Ela come back with a small wooden stool and a pair of rosy cheeks. Before I knew it, she had pulled her sweater over her head and was twisting her thick hair up in a bun, leaving me to gawk at her thin but defined upper arms shown off by her dark red tank top. And now the owner of that beautiful body sat down only a few inches away from me.

Again, I scooted forward, silently pleading that she wouldn't find me revolting after all, and began running my palms over her neck. With every minute that I heard Ela sigh and felt her rub against my hand like a cat, I felt more confident that my touch was welcome, and so I dared to lean into her so I could apply more pressure.

"Did they teach you that at a trade school, too?"

"Nope, but our garage offers free back rubs to our favourite customers with every car inspection."

"Do you now?" Ela smirked at me over her shoulder. "Let me guess, all of your favourite customers are female and age-graded forty."

"Now that is company policy and therefore confidential," I grinned back before I realized what we were doing: Ela and I were flirting. Clearly, she was in more need of human connection than I'd thought. There was no other explanation for why she would smile at me this way.

"Uh-huh," I hastily cleared my throat and ran my hands along her arms again, "have you ever met other people with such… powers?"

"No, and I have no idea how I would find them either. 'Superheroes Anonymous', wouldn't that be something?" she added with a wry chuckle, making me laugh as well. "If it were at least a useful power," she continued more softly, "but I can't even light a fire out of nothing, only burn living creatures. All I can do is hurt others."

"Perhaps not anymore," I told her, eager to keep her in good spirits. "We need to test if you can touch other people now, too, perhaps at the store. Very carefully," I hurried to add when she flinched and her terrified face met mine over her shoulder. "Listen, I get that you're scared. You don't want to hurt anyone else and find out that your karma is still bad, but at the same time you want to know, don't you?"

"O- of course I do."

"Then let's go to the store tomorrow. Get into a crowded spot and take off a glove. If you only touch someone really quickly, it should only sting and not burn, right?"

"Right," Ela's drawn-out answer came after a moment. "OK," she shook herself out of her fear at last, "let's do it tomorrow after breakfast. We need some fresh fruit anyway."

"I'm proud of you!"

And she willingly let herself be pulled close to me. What a great fit. And she'd said 'we'. I couldn't wait for her to find out her curse, karma or whatever it was had lifted. What if it had, though? As much as I wished for her to break free, what would it mean for us? I wasn't and wouldn't be anywhere close to my goal weight anytime soon, and as little as I liked to admit it to myself, I needed Ela and her healthy, isolated lifestyle. Back in the city, close to candy stores and burger joints, I could relapse anytime. It was selfish but I needed her to myself just for a while longer.

All throughout dinner, which for the first time we ate not sitting across from each other but at a 90°-angle, I made sure I never broke physical contact for long, playing barefoot footsie with Ela or brushing along her bare arms. Now that her secret was out, conversation flowed and we caught up on weeks' worth of conversation and laughter. Finally, I got a full view of that side of her I had only glimpsed so far: witty, full of stories and quick to burst out laughing. After dinner, we retreated to the couch where we laid down and I pulled her as close to me as I could. None of this was wise but all of it was right.

When neither of us was able to hold back the yawns anymore, Ela finally stretched and scooted away, although never breaking contact since my belly immediately followed after her. Being super fat sometimes has unexpected perks.

"I don't want to leave. What if I wake up and can't touch you again?"

I couldn't make out Ela's face in the shadows caused by the single thick candle she had lit earlier but I had no doubt her face matched her words. Still, it would be hard enough to explain to Silke that I had spent weeks in a woman's house without anything happening between us, but even tougher should she ever find out we spent a night together. Not that I planned on telling her but if she asked, she would read the truth in my face at once. I had never been able to lie to her. And yet… Ela needed me right now. It was a no-brainer.

"Would you like to sleep on the couch with me tonight?"

Instantly she sat up, shaking her head so violently that her hair swayed like a dark curtain. "Absolutely not. What if my condition returns and I'll burn you? You'll be scarred forever."

Chuckling, I struggled into a sitting position as well. "For one thing, I already am – haven't you seen the stretch marks? For another, I don't think it will come back. But more importantly: I'll take the risk."

"But I won't."

"Too bad, this is my decision."

My face might be a liability at a poker table but I had yet to find someone who could outstare me. Plus, it helped that Ela was not only up against me but also herself as well. "OK," she finally relented, failing to suppress a smile.

When Ela returned with freshly brushed teeth, dressed only in a tank top and shorts that showed off her perfect legs, I suddenly realized that having her beside me during the night would mean taking off my pants and reveal my sagging gut. It was nothing she hadn't seen before but that experience didn't exactly beg for a repetition.

"All yours," she nodded in the direction of the bathroom, brushing her hand along my arm.

I only nodded. In the bathroom, I took my nerves out on my teeth until I spat blood into the sink but still hadn't come up with a solution or excuse. When I joined Ela, she was lying on her stomach underneath my huge duvet, a goofy smile on her face that morphed into the nervous kind when her eyes connected with mine, then the rest of me before she averted her red face. She'd never looked at me the way she just had. What was that? Well, whatever it was, she wouldn't feel it for much longer.

"Uh, Ela," I began, coming to a standstill about two feet away from the couch, "I'm not very... I mean... you might feel— "

"Never assume anything," she waved away the rest of my sentence with a stern face, "right now you couldn't be more perfect."

'Right now,', true. To someone with her condition I would indeed be temporarily perfect but if it turned out tomorrow that she could touch people again, she'd change her mind in a heartbeat. This was perhaps the only night I'd ever spend with her, so I'd better make sure I keep her attitude towards me intact until tomorrow and use my body to make her feel as good as I could.

"Uh, OK. Still, could you..." I broke off, my face in flames.

"Of course." Quickly she turned on her side, her back to me, to give me a bit of privacy while I slid off my sweats. Immediately my belly flowed out and hung free. So freaking embarrassing. Struggling to push those thoughts away, I slipped under the duvet and rearranged my body for Ela. "Ready."

Wordlessly she scooted closer until the mass be-tween us refused to be compacted any further, and I placed my arms around her as much as was possible.

"Is that OK?" a small voice asked after a while.

"Yes." As long as it didn't gross her out that she could feel my hanging gut against the back of her thighs.

Now her head turned. "Are you sure? Because I don't want you to feel like you have to do this just because I'm skin-contact deprived. You must tell me if I'm making you uncomfortable."

She was but I'd be dammed if I told her. "You're fine." And I pulled her even closer for emphasis, hoping my fat arms wouldn't keep her from breath-ing properly. God only knew how much one of them weighed. At least I was clean and smelled fresh but there wasn't anything I could do about my size.

Unlike earlier, we didn't speak this time. Lying like this with her was torture, sweet and painful at the same time. She smelled so uniquely of herself and her legs went on for much longer than I was used to. I'd been in love with Silke's body but, while she would only date big guys, I'd always enjoyed women of all sizes. Well, not recently, not in a long time, and feeling Ela against me now and breathing her in was turning out to be more than I could handle. I needed to turn on my right side.

Oh damn. If I did, I'd be sure to gross her out with my fat sloshing around and the couch creaking. It was no use, though, I couldn't keep lying like this. I began to shift and after the usual amount of groaning on both my and the couch's part, I finally lay on my right and everything was in place again. Only a moment later I felt motion behind me before a slender arm snaked around my side, gliding over all the rolls. A second after I felt pressure against my giant butt.

I hated how defensive I felt about my body now. I'd never minded being a big guy and always had a retort ready but ever since even an FFA like Silke had turned from me in disgust, I'd finally opened my eyes to what I had become. The contented sigh behind me and the brush of her fingers on my arm did nothing to change the truth.

CHAPTER TWELVE
Ela: Experiment

Although in terms of actual sleep last night's ranged in the flop ten of my life, the sensation under my fingertips marked it as one that would stay committed to memory forever: skin. To be exact, a large, chubby hand on top of mine. What my sleep-deprived brain and hesitant fingers reported to be attached to said hand instantly brought a smile to my lips: Blake had stayed with me all night and I was still able to touch him.

"Morning," a gravelly voice behind me roused me fully, causing me to shift until I faced its owner.

"Morning. Uh-huh, you didn't get much sleep either, did you?"

The tired, round face in front of me stretched into a lazy smile. "Meaning I look like hell, thanks a lot."

"Well, considering how I feel, I probably do, too."

"You couldn't if you tried," Blake chuckled, his hand searching for mine under the duvet. "And in case you were about to suggest never to repeat this, think again."

I could only stare at him in wonder. The last night *had* taken its toll on him and yet none other than his swollen-eyed, stubbled face would have felt so right beside me. "You're amazing, you know that?"

"Yeah," he smirked and reached up to run his thick, warm fingers through my hair and down my neck. While his curls were begging me to return the favour, the past three years had left their mark on me, and despite the knowledge that Blake was immune to my condition, my hands stopped inches away from his hair. Suddenly his hand reappeared from under the duvet and gently placed my fingers into his soft curls. After a moment I felt my brain reengage and issue the command to release the breath I had been holding. Then my fingers slowly travelled down his stubbly cheek, down past his double chin and even further, over the fabric of his voluminous T-shirt and back onto the silky skin of his upper arms.

This time it was Blake's turn to expel a breath as my fingertips glided over the series of rolls. Here he was, with enough body mass for three people so he would last me for a long time whereas a skinny athlete would have been stroked out in half an hour at the most. I had meant it yesterday: he couldn't be more perfect, and not only because he was the first person I was able to touch in three years. Although I was still coming to terms with my physical ideals, there was no denying that Blake fulfilled them perfectly. With every movement during the night, his bulk had shifted and settled into a new set of rolls and bulges. His body was like a kaleidoscope, different with every turn, and always with a new arrangement to discover.

Hunger and anticipation about the impending experiment in town, however, soon propelled me out of bed and Blake followed to help me with breakfast. All throughout the – silent – preparations I couldn't stop casting furtive looks in his direction. What if one night was all I was granted and when I touched him next he would yell and yank his hand away?

"Hey."

Apparently, my looks hadn't been that furtive after all, for Blake waddled over from the fridge to where I was standing by the table and pulled me into his arms. Limp with relief that he was still immune, I snuggled into his softness and breathed him in. Just what I needed. If only I could breathe him in for the next year or so.

"I'm sure the curse won't come back for me, and if you need to keep touching me to believe it, feel free." Automatically, my arms tightened around what I could reach of him. "And whatever will happen in town later, I'm not going anywhere as long as you want me here, OK?"

"OK." Then I pulled away from him abruptly. "I don't want you to have to ride in the cargo area again." The non sequitur caused Blake's eyebrows to crawl up his forehead. "Not only because it's illegal but because I also hate it. I want you beside me, so let's take the bus."

His face softened as if he was touched I wanted to spare his feelings when in truth my heart had gone out to him every time I had watched him climb into the rear.

"Thank you." Again, his thick arms contracted around me, the sensation of sinking into his pliable flesh almost causing me to press my lips to the silky skin on his neck.

An hour later we were walking towards the bus station. It was slow progress but if that's what it took for Blake to regain his health, I was more than ready to adjust. Plus, there was the fact that each minute delayed the dreaded moment of truth. Every time my mind riffled through possible outcomes, I yanked it back into the present with resolve. If I let myself dwell on the ramifications, I might very well bolt in panic and shut myself in my bedroom like a child. I had to take this one step at a time, much like Blake.

Despite my preoccupation, I couldn't help but notice how each passenger's eyes snapped to us the minute we entered the bus and the sensation was as novel as it was discomfiting. Naturally, I had received my share of curious looks due to my height, or when I dressed like a goth but never had I found myself on the receiving end of that particular gamut of human emotions: incredulity, revulsion and ridicule. Even though they were directed at my companion and not at me, I felt the familiar prickles in my face and kept my eyes firmly first on the astounded-looking driver and then on my ticket.

"Uh-huh, Ela?"

At that moment I had no option but to force my eyes up and to take in Blake's red face.

"You go ahead. I- I don't fit through the turnstile, so I have to enter through the rear door."

Again, the ramifications of his obesity hit me like a truck. All morning I had worried about nobody but myself while Blake dealt with his issues every day *silently*. With his shoulders sagging and his crimson face averted, he looked at the image of embarrassment and isolation. While I had always striven to avoid the former, I was basically on a first-name basis with the latter and I couldn't bear for anyone to have to make that acquaintance, too. When I had insisted we take the bus, it was to *spare* him discomfort, not add to it. As if controlled by an outside force, I straightened my spine and fixed my gaze on his face.

"Not a chance, I'm coming with you. Let's go," I prodded him when the driver opened his mouth to put in his two cent's worth, grabbed Blake's hand and led him out of the bus.

In my job I had cultivated and honed the skill of the evil eye, and although I had used it but rarely since then, in the instant, we re-entered it reported back for duty with a proud salute. The moment my glare collided with two whispering septuagenarians, the ladies startled and sought visual refuge in their purses. I mowed down everyone in our line of vision until Blake carefully lowered himself onto a double seat and me into a single one facing him. His cheeks were still splotched with red but as soon as I took off my gloves, placed my elbows on my knees and slid my hands back into his, a smile slow-ly caused the splotches to fade like clouds in the sun.

His chubby fingers responded to the caress my own thinner digits administered, and although I had initially intended to *offer* comfort, I suddenly felt as if his touch infused me with some strength of its own. He was what mattered, not the crowd of judgmental strangers around us. However, the ex-periment would turn out, I had just proven I could overcome some of my opportunistic attitudes. Alt-hough our hands disengaged when I leaned back, we kept our knees in close contact.

Fifteen silent but strangely intimate minutes later, we entered the Aldi parking lot, not holding hands but walking close. I offered to get a shopping cart while Blake waited at the entrance since he couldn't comfortably plot between the poles of the rack that held the carts in place. Usually, they were arranged in one long caterpillar-like line but today the meagre number left gave evidence to the crowd in the store that I needed. Due to my condition I usually chose times when very few shoppers were present but to-day I needed plenty of people around me that I could blame in case the experiment failed.

Just as I was drawing closer to Blake with my cart, an unshaven, haggard stretch of a youngster in jeans and a leather jacket moved to enter the store in long, hurried strides.

"Move it, fat-ass!"

Poor Blake. This experiment was turning out to be as much of a trial for him as for me. Gritting my teeth, I jerked my head at the offender. "I'd say we have our most deserving candidate."

Blake's face, bright red again, looked as if it couldn't decide what to do. At last, he cleared his throat. "I agree. Let's do this. Either you can touch him now, or if you can't, he'll get what he deserves. Win-win," he added with a grim smile.

He took over the cart, leaving me to admire both his courage and his broad shape from behind. While I might not dare act on my preferences yet, be it in private or in public, I could enjoy his figure surreptitiously. Mr Leatherjacket, meanwhile, hadn't progressed very far. Currently, he was pushing his way through a small crowd of people towards the doughnuts on sale. Perfect. As quickly as I could I made my way past Blake, who was taking up the majority of the aisle and joined the doughnut crowd. Then I deliberately stretched out my un-gloved fingers to graze them along the man's arm. This was it, the moment of truth.

"Ow! What the hell?!"

Clutching his arm, the youngster whirled around in the midst of suddenly staring faces, his menacing scowl zooming in on me, and stepped closer. His clothes reeked of tobacco and his teeth were at nodding acquaintance with a toothbrush at best. Although still reeling from the shock that my bad karma was still very much effective, my acting skills immediately kicked in.

"Oh dear, what happened?"

"That's what I'm asking you!" a gust of tobacco-contaminated oxygen insulted my nostrils, "you burned me!"

"With what? Do you see a cigarette around here somewhere?"

The guy looked confused for a moment but stepped closer still, causing me to move backwards out of harm's way. "If you touch me, I'll scream bloody murder."

Why would none of the gawking customers come to my rescue? Just when my aggressor opened his foul mouth again, I felt a looming presence behind me. "Seriously, if you touch her, I'll sit on you."

The man's narrowed eyes darted over to Blake behind me, widening as if at a loss how he could have missed the most conspicuous person at the store drawing closer. At last, he gulped and withdrew, muttered expletives scattering in his wake while our fellow shoppers averted their faces in evident discomfort. A moment later, I felt myself being pulled into a tight embrace from behind. Although I gratefully registered the warmth of Blake's thick fingers on my skin, the motion only served to drive home the point that he was still the only one immune to my condition.

When I let us back inside the house 45 minutes later, I only dimly recalled how I had ridden home seated in a row of four seats with Blake beside me, his arm around my shoulders as far as it would go. After we had stored away from the few things we had bought, I turned to him.

"Blake? Will, you lay down with me and hold me for a while?"

He only nodded and walked me over to the couch where he lay down on his right, arranged his spreading bulk with red cheeks and pulled me close with my back against his massive belly. For once not even a muscle thought to wiggle closer or touch his skin, and thus lying motionless I finally allowed the events of the past hour to penetrate the protective shields that had sprung up around me at the store.

"I told myself not to get my hopes up but I did."

"I know."

Blake's arm tightened around me, only it did nothing to alleviate the intensifying despair. What now? Should I regret ever finding out that I could touch him, and from now on bury all hope at normalcy? Or should I try someone else? The mere thought rang of people screaming in pain and the clang of a psych-ward door. And even if I did find someone else who was immune, how long would it last? How long would it last with Blake? And would I ever function in normal society again? Perhaps it was for the better that I stayed put. I was safe here in my tiny, familiar world. Forever.

Suddenly it was as if a dam had broken. A sob escaped me, another and another, an unpreventable mass breakout of sobs.

"You- you know the most p- pathetic thing? A part of me felt relieved just now that it didn't work! Relieved that I c- could stay where I w- was, safely tucked away! I mean, at f- first I panicked that the bad k- karma was still in place, but then I th- thought, what if I've f- forgotten how to be among people? I've l- lived alone for so long that I have no idea if I could f- fit in anywhere again. And even if I manage to b- build another life for myself some- where, wh- what if the bad karma comes back? I don't know if I c- could go through all that again!"

That last part drowned in a new wail. Sob after sob shook me until I felt every bone in my body and my raw throat and eyes threw in the towel. On- ly then did the sensation of a warm, soothing mo- tion on my scalp penetrate my teary haze and I slowly gave myself up to the gentle caress.

"You're not pathetic," its author's equally gentle voice drifted over at some point, "it's totally under- standable that you'd be scared. Anyone would be."

'Anyone'. At that moment I realized Blake was not merely using phrases to comfort me but that he dealt with his own fear every day, a fear of relapses, rejection by friends and family and failure to re- claim his job. Except for the one time when I had hugged him, however, he had never complained but silently kept on working towards his goal. A wave of admiration and gratefulness for his presence broke over my head, flooding out everything that had been dragging me down into that dark place I knew so well. I might have saved his life there on the bridge but in a way, he was also saving mine.

"Thank you. For everything."

"Don't sweat it. By the way," I caught a hint of a smile in his voice, "you're one hell of an actress.

Not only getting that guy at the store off your scent but also actually making him feel bad for snapping at you? Nice job."

"Thanks," I felt myself smiling back even though a moment ago it seemed I would never do so again. "You weren't so bad either. Where other people would announce an imminent punch, you threaten the guy with *sitting* on him."

"Well, coming from me that is way more threatening than a sorry punch."

What do you know, not only did my face remember how to smile, but also I hadn't forgotten how to laugh either? It felt so good to exchange silly jokes with Blake about his weight. Despite his being at a low point in life, he always seemed so confident and at peace with himself – not with his weight but with himself as a person. No, I could never regret finding out that he was the only one immune. As little as we both felt we had to give, we could offer each other comfort and acceptance. Automatically my body wiggled closer, feeling his flab mould around me and his arm contract. As though with a will of its own, my nose began to graze the skin on his heavy arm, breathing in his scent, and at some point my lips joined in, pressing a light kiss to the silky inside of his arm.

"Is this OK?"

"You-" Blake cleared his throat, "you don't have to keep asking. I'll tell you when it's not, alright?"

"Uh-huh, OK, but I have to ask one thing in general: would you mind if I touched more of you? More besides your hands and arms, I mean?"

"Are you sure about that?" he murmured after a moment. "The image of me naked must give you nightmares already."

"Please don't talk like that. I really mean it, I would like to touch more of you, but only if it doesn't make you uncomfortable." Again, silence behind me. "Uh-huh, never mind."

How utterly embarrassing. First, I dissolve into tears and then I practically beg him to strip for me again. I'd better put some healthy distance between us right now—

"Wait." A strong hand held my shoulder and kept me still. "Yes, you may touch me."

"No," I shook my head, trying to pull out of his grasp, "I'm asking too much and making you uncomfortable—"

"Ela, shut up." His firm yet gentle command caused me to freeze. "I want this, too. Would... uh-huh, would my back be OK?"

"More than OK," I responded after a moment, feeling another smile bloom on my cheeks that he would not only accept but also welcome my touch.

I waited to let him shift and remove his T-shirt in privacy before I turned, discovering that he had pulled it over his head but was holding it protectively against his ample front. Although I had seen his back before, the sight of all the bulges and creases brought me up shortly before I felt the by now familiar throb between my thighs again. Every time I realized that his body was indeed attractive to me, it was easier to admit it to myself, and at this moment another sensation set in: the absence of any guilt. How could something that was in our nature be wrong or shameful? If people came in all shapes and sizes, why shouldn't the same be true for attraction?

"Is that OK for you?" I murmured while I glided over each wave and roll gently. "Sorry, I keep forgetting I don't have to ask."

Again, Blake cleared his throat "It's fine. And yeah, it's OK. For you?"

"Again, more than OK," I smiled at him, hoping that hearing it in my voice would provide sufficient reassurance, "thank you for letting me do this. It means a lot to me."

He laughed at that, sending ripples down his vast body and more moisture into my panties. "If gratefulness is what you're feeling when you touch me, I'm all yours."

"Clearly you don't believe me but I mean it. When I touch you, it's as if I'm part of the world again. You have no idea what it's like to live isolated for so long, connected with other people only through the internet. Sometimes I feel as if there is only a digital version of me, like an avatar." However, I couldn't allow him to think that this was the only reason. "But that's not all," I smiled at his back again, tracing one of his creases with my finger. "You feel good. You have amazing skin."

"Yeah, only too much of it."

That was a tricky one. From a health and mobility perspective I had to agree but not when it came to what I felt for him. "I still like it."

When he didn't respond, I simply blocked out everything but the sensation underneath my fingers. He was here now, willing to let me grab, knead and even kiss, so do that I would. That lower throbbing intensified into a hum as I grabbed fistfuls of Blake's smooth flesh and alternately kissed, sucked and even bit into the plush mass, my breathing driving out every other sound. No, actually that wasn't true. Blake' panting was ringing in my ears just as loudly as my own. He was enjoying it! All this time I had assumed he was still pining after Silke, but he certainly wasn't engaged in any pining at the moment. In fact, he'd told me 'I'm all yours', and right now I wanted him to be mine, no matter the consequences. Slowly but with resolve, I proceeded by kneading his doughy shoulders and kissing my way up to his neck.

"Ela?"

He sounded as if my fingers were choking instead of caressing his neck. "Ela, please stop." His fingers slipped over mine, holding them in place. "Please, this isn't what you really want."

WTF? How would he know what I—

"You're just overwhelmed. Please, I don't want you to do anything you might regret. Also, I'm not ready."

It was that last whisper that caused my fingers and mouth to abandon their target at once. I had specifically asked him to stop me when he felt uncomfortable, so I had no right to be mad, which didn't mean I wasn't entitled to a deep, most likely beet-root-coloured mortification instead. If I had thought my actions embarrassing before, I had now ascended – or rather descended – to a whole new level of patheticism. If there was any chance of us remaining housemates with a semblance of dignity and normalcy between us, I had to extricate myself now under the plea of temporary insanity, apologize and let the air cool off between us through an extended walk. However, a soft but unyielding sensation around my wrist forestalled any such extrication effort.

Blake shifted himself into a sitting position with an effort, his body mass wobbling while he struggled back into his T-shirt, a sight which drew my eyes like a laser pointer a cat. When his head emerged from the hole and his eyes caught mine on his body, he tugged the enormous piece of fabric into place with a crimson face but redirected his gaze to my face while he availed himself of both my hands.

"Don't be mad and please don't be embarrassed either. What you just did…" his eyes closed for a moment, "let's just say if circumstances were different, I would have RSVP'd to your invitation in a heartbeat." His phrasing tickled a smile out of me, to which he responded with an utterly endearing one of his own. "I know you were about to head out but please let's go together. No more running, OK?"

"You're right."

'If circumstances were different'. Throughout our slow progress through the woods, Blake's words ricocheted in my mind. What circumstances? If he were thin? If he weren't still in love with his ex? If I looked more like his ex? If I were normal?

At last, we arrived at the chain-link fence that ran along this part of the river because of the dangerous rapids. It had taken us at least twice as long than it would have had I walked by myself but for a man of Blake's size it was still an admirable feat, and I told him so.

"Thanks," he panted back at me, wiping his forehead, "you were right, daily walks are a great workout."

Not another word was exchanged when his arms slid around my waist and he pulled me against him from behind. For a while, all we did was stare at the rushing water in its seasonal garb of depressing brown. Also, my eyes kept straying to the bridge increasingly.

"Did you mean to do it?"

While I hadn't intended to blurt out that particular question, I did long to know the answer. At last, I heard and felt a deep breath behind me.

"I tried but as it turns out, hypothermia isn't the best way to go when you've got layers and layers of natural padding."

I turned in his embrace. "Have you always been able to joke about yourself?"

A smile lit up his round face at that and suddenly I struggled to suppress a moan.

"Since I've always been big, yeah, pretty much."

How enviable. I had never been able to enjoy a laugh at my own expense. It had been hard enough being taken seriously as a woman in a competitive industry, and shaping myself into who I'd believed I had to become hadn't let any room for self-deprecating humour. I had been an opportunist, plain and simple. Not so Blake. No matter what mood he was in, he was confident enough to be himself.

"I don't understand how a funny, confident guy like you would see no other way but suicide."

"Well," he began after another protracted moment of silence, "when you watch everything slip out of your control and then lose the person you thought was the most important one in your life, the one you thought would always have your back..."

I failed to suppress a stab of unwarranted jealousy but my mind also snagged on the 'you thought' part. Did that mean the – sturdy – pedestal he had so far kept Silke on was vacant or in the process of being vacated? But something else was pressing on my mind even more urgently.

"But did you actually mean to do it? Did you come out to the bridge that day to kill yourself?"

I had hate to remind him of his darkest moment but I wanted no more secrets between us. Well, aside from the fact that I was hopelessly in lust with him. If there was a sliver of a chance for something to happen, we needed to trust each other.

"Coming to the bridge wasn't part of any plan," Blake began on a mighty exhale. "When Silke screamed me out of her apartment, I simply took the bus that happened to be waiting by the curb and rode it to the last stop. From there I just stumbled onward, not really seeing where I was going." He paused. "But yes, once I recognized the opportunity, I meant to take it."

Reflexively, I pulled his arms closer around me. If I had driven by only thirty minutes later… why though would he choose a public road for a relatively slow suicide method? Blake, meanwhile, seemed to sense my question.

"Actually, I meant to jump off the bridge but as it turned out, I was too fat to climb over the parapet. How pathetic is that, huh?"

This time his laugh was entirely devoid of humour. It took me a while to process that new bit of information before I turned in his arms again to look at his red-cheeked face. "You're not pathetic. You have a problem but you're working on it."

A slowly unfurling smile was my reward and he raised his chin to kiss my knit-covered forehead. "And so are you. Don't give up. If the bad karma has lifted for me, chances are good it will for other people, too. Maybe it just takes more time or a different person. Or perhaps it'll fade first for people that deserve it," he added with a grin.

"Perhaps you're right."

The more I mulled that thought over, the more plausible it seemed. That fat-phobic jerk at the store, who had most likely accumulated enough bad karma of his own, certainly did not belong among the deserving. Already the future looked brighter.

"Thank you."

I closed my eyes and I leaned back against him, pulling his arms tighter around me still. Why on earth had Silke given up on him? He was a keeper.

CHAPTER THIRTEEN

Blake: Choices

Even after Ela had done as I'd asked her and gone back to the house on her own, I could still feel her imprint on me, the same way I remembered exactly what her hands had done on my back earlier. There had been no doubt about it, she'd been getting ready to jump me and she would have if I hadn't stopped her. That she would need someone close was understandable after years of isolation but that she would throw herself on me was a whole different story. Granted, she hadn't had sex in three years but I'd always thought sexual urges weren't as bad for women as for men. Were they, though, and was Ela's need so strong that she would even do me? Whenever I thought I understood that woman better, I took a step backwards.

Should I take forward steps with her at all, though? Even with Silke drifting further and further out of my reach – and to be honest, my thoughts as well – this thing between Ela and me was just temporary, messed-up emotions in an extreme situation. Powerful emotions, though. I'd almost lost it when she'd broken down crying. She always seemed so strong, so in charge, but for all her self-sufficiency she was someone who needed to feel sheltered. That was a first for me. Silke was a tough and confident woman and, except for cuddling with her after a hard day at work, she had rarely needed my protection.

I could so well relate to Ela's fear of life in society. For me, it wasn't that I was afraid of people but afraid of all the unhealthy food available at every corner. Who knew if I would ever learn to eat right and get down to a decent weight? And if I did, what if I fell back into my old habits? In a way Ela and I were in the same boat – with her side lifted out of the water, I grinned to myself. Was I a bad person for feeling a tiny bit relieved that her experiment hadn't worked?

If she came on to me again as she had, I might not be able to stop her, especially when chances were high she would spend the night with me on the couch again. Of course, I could ask her to sleep in her own bed. Yes, I could do that.

Oh, who was I kidding, of course, I wouldn't. Damn it, how could something so wrong, be so right?

Half sitting up, half reclining on the couch was a comfortable position for me and one in which Ela could cuddle up next to me perfectly. For once I did what I had excelled at for years and blocked out all thought what she might think about my size. She hadn't stopped smiling since she had curled up on my left and placed one hand on my belly underneath my T-shirt, so who was I to question her decision?

Again, conversation flowed easily between us. What was new, though, was that for the first time we made plans together like me showing her how to use the new car-cleaning products that had arrived the other day, or she teaching me things at the computer. Granted, they were about the smallest plans two people can make but the only ones I could allow myself to consider. The moment of bigger decisions came, though, when Ela began to yawn whilst she turned to me.

"Uh-huh, I guess I'm going to bed."

Her eyes remained on mine, a mute plea to invite her to spend the night next to me again but the fact that she didn't ask outright meant she was giving me an out. I knew I should take it. I was getting in too deep. So far, I had soaked up everything, each touch and each sigh of appreciation, but I couldn't let myself get used to them, nor delude myself that they stemmed from anything but lack of alternatives for her. I should be grateful she showed no signs of revulsion.

"Want to sleep here again?"

Aw, crap. Apparently, my gut had just made the decision, just as it always had over the past years, only its decisions had so far been restricted to food choices. Now it was making *life* choices. Ten minutes later we lay close together in the dark again like we had the night before, only Ela's fingertips had slipped underneath my T-shirt, lightly grazing over my fat love handle. Just like on the couch earlier, I let her and chose to enjoy rather than to question it.

"What would you do with your life if your karma got back to normal?"

"I'd like to help people," Ela's voice drifted over to me after a moment. "Perhaps become a therapist."

"I think you'd make a great therapist. You're a good listener."

"Thank you." Silence. "Or maybe a massage therapist or a chiropractor – something where I could make people feel *good* by touching them."

Ela touching other people, other *men*, for a living – now that I didn't want to picture. I knew I had no right to jealousy, which didn't help one bit, though. Instead, I chose to focus on our conversation.

"Whatever you choose, you'll be amazing at it."

"Thank you for saying that."

"What about your plans for your private life?"

"I'd love to travel again." Again she paused. "What are *your* plans for when you're down to a healthy weight?"

'When', not 'if'. For her, there seemed to be no doubt about it. Me, I wasn't so sure.

"Also travel."

Even though I wasn't sure I'd ever get down to a size that didn't require buying two aeroplane seats, I'd gladly pay for them if it meant not missing out any longer. Silke wasn't just afraid of flying, she was afraid of heights in general, so for the past five years, I'd been missing out on vacations outside of driving or train distance, or even going up on viewing platforms. Being afraid of heights wasn't her fault and it was wrong to blame her for it, yet I did.

Argh! Thoughts of her definitely had no place in his bed!

"Where would you go?" Ela's soft voice interrupted my swirling thoughts, her fingers lightly squeezing my flesh. How was I supposed to carry on a conversation like this?

"Uh-huh, the U.S. My English sucks but I've always wanted to visit San Francisco."

"Me too!" she gasped and came up on her elbow. "I've explored the east coast pretty well already but I've never been to California." She paused, her eyes futilely searching for mine in the darkness. "I could come with you and help you out English-wise."

"You'd want to take a trip with me?"

"Sure, why not?"

This was pure speculation here, right? Right??

"Uh, that is if you could bear a control freak with you for two or three weeks," she added, her voice shrinking in on itself.

"I'm sure you wouldn't be if the curses were gone," I smiled at her and pulled her back into her earlier lying position.

"At least less so," she laughed and snuggled close again. "I'm sure you would like Oman, too, and I bet you're amazing at bartering on bazaars."

"I actually am. How did you know?"

"Just a feeling."

And her hand slipped back underneath my T-shirt with a deep sigh. If she kept this up, her touches and her appreciation of me as a person, there was no way I would resist her the next time she wanted to have her way with me. That just couldn't happen, though, not when I still hadn't worked out how I felt about Silke. We'd been together for five years, dammit, and I couldn't just turn off my feelings. Of course, I didn't know Silke's side of the story. Three weeks had passed since our breakup; did she miss me or had she moved on? I almost laughed out loud; me mentally chasing after one woman while another one's hands were groping me when I probably had a shot with neither.

The next morning after breakfast, Ela recorded another YouTube video in her room. Normally she would kick me out for that but it was pouring outside and she only nodded when I promised her I would put in my earphones and get busy at the computer. It wasn't a lie. Besides, what was the point of eavesdropping when I would see the results on YouTube soon anyway? As soon as I had booted up my laptop, I clicked on Silke's Facebook page. She hadn't unfriended me even though her relationship status was now set to 'single'. Not taking the time to dwell on those two contradicting facts, I moved on to recent photos. There were some friends I recognized but also eight pictures of her with a guy I'd never seen before. A chubby guy.

To be honest, I had no clue how I felt right now, I only knew I needed to get out of here, rain or no rain. Somehow the option of raiding the fridge only surfaced briefly at the back of my mind. At that moment, Ela emerged from her bedroom, her phone in hand and her cheeks pink, the way they only turned when she felt embarrassed. What on earth had that video been about?

"Uh, in case you'd like to get started with video editing, I was going to take a walk anyway." I raised my hand in a vague waving gesture. "A lot on my mind."

Her eyes seemed to search my face. "I can tell," she nodded at last.

Despite my preoccupation, I couldn't help but feel touched. However selfish and shallow she may have been in the past, the Ela I had come to know was intuitive and emphatic like no one else I had ever met.

The act of walking never failed to rub in my face how long and rocky the path to a healthy life still was but at the same time it always put things in perspective, too: whatever my feelings about Silke, it was no use speculating about her side of the story. She'd made it clear she wanted me to concentrate on myself right now and she was right about that. Even Ela had to take a backseat. I had to do what was best for me. When I entered the house sometime later, Ela was just getting ready to head out herself. Perfect. With any luck, today's video would be online already.

Bingo.

"Have you ever felt as if you're drying up inside and getting more unattractive by the day? Nobody has touched you in months, not even you? Well, even if you think that you're the last person to deserve to be touched, you're not. Pleasuring yourself is something you never have to earn. Do it, and do it as often as you want, without shame. Try as many toys, techniques, perhaps your hands or the shower head, but never stop. Do it at least twice a week and whenever you're feeling particularly undesirable.

"Also, explore your fantasies, especially those outside the norm. Perhaps you're into pain, perhaps you're into threesomes. You might be into women, short guys, bald guys or heavy guys. Dismiss no possibility. Whatever your preference, you don't have to be ashamed of it. You don't have to go public with it but you never have to hide it from yourself either. Have you ever considered that sexual preferences might be as colourful as the people around you? Seriously, anything goes, as long as you don't hurt yourself or other people. Well, unless you're into SM but even that has healthy limits."

That last part made me laugh.

"Try it, try everything. And if you're not on friendly terms with your body, take a shower first and use your favourite products. Make yourself feel as good about yourself as you can before you make yourself feel even better with the greatest gift of nature to us. Even if you have the feeling that you stood last in line for everything good, this is the one thing nobody can take away from you. Be good to yourself, and to others. Remember: Karma is only a bitch if you are."

WTF? While I'd been sure Ela's physical reaction to my body was just her being overwhelmed and lonely, now she was giving other single women advice about exploring if they were into 'heavy guys'? Was that just an example or did it mean something more? I knew I should probably hang an 'off-limits' sign around her neck to remind me but this latest revelation made me question everything since her our first touch.

Ela noticed, of course. All through lunch preparations I couldn't stop staring at her as if her cryptic YouTube comment was spelt out on her face in plain German.

"Blake, what is it?"

"Hmm?"

"You're staring at me."

"Sorry, just a lot on my mind."

Those onions did keep me occupied for some time, my eyes more so than I would have wished, but again they kept drifting over to the woman beside me.

"Seriously, what is it?"

"I..." hastily I cleared my throat, "sometimes it's just difficult to take in how you're coping with all this. I mean, you have no idea what brought on this condition and what can make it go away and yet you're handling it. In my case, it's all in my hands and still, I'm frustrated as hell. I don't know how you do it."

Although a pretext, it wasn't a lie either. I hated getting out of breath so fast, how much I sweated and how long everything took. I missed the mobility.

Ela's hands had paused in the act of dicing veggies, and suddenly I heard her gasp. "I've just had an idea—uh, no, I haven't. Never mind."

"Hey," I reached out to turn her by the shoulder, "what's wrong? What was your idea?"

"I… I was thinking the local ice rink might be something for you because skating is easy on the joints, but then I remembered why I can't go: accidents and doctor visits."

"You think *you're* the problem?" I scoffed, caught between bitterness and amusement, "what makes you think *I* can skate?"

"Didn't you grow up with ice rinks and skates or at least roller blades? Most Germans can skate."

"Most *thin* Germans."

Again she coloured. Crap, now I'd made her uncomfortable again when she was one of the few people believing in my abilities at all. Her absolute confidence that I could do anything, even as a super fat guy, still threw me. Again I touched her shoulder.

"I'm sorry. Sometimes I get a little caught up in myself. Uh, how are *you* at ice-skating?"

"I used to be decent. I even still have a pair of skates."

"Me too." In some by now neatly packed and la-belled box. "Have you ever broken a bone or twist-ed an ankle when you skated?"

"No. Fallen on my butt, yes, but not often."

The more I thought about her idea, the more I warmed to it. "How about it then? We could pick a time when not too many people will be around and the risk of accidents will be minimal. I have no idea if I can still skate or if my skates will hold me but I want to try, and I think you should, too. You need some fun, urgently. I really think it's going to work; everyone will be fully covered except for their faces, so unless you plan on kissing someone other than me, you should be fine."

No freaking way, where had that last part come from?! Then again, the more I thought about *that* idea, the more I warmed to it, too.

CHAPTER FOURTEEN

Ela: Ice and fire

The local indoor ice rink, which had been modernized three years ago and attracted skaters from a twenty-mile radius, catered to more than just teenage clients: as the website informed me, every Monday they reserved a time slot from 10 to 12 AM to senior citizens, although a call to the management revealed that they would welcome someone younger but with special needs as well.

When Blake and I made our way out of the locker area where we had changed into our skates, the elderly but nonetheless athletic clientele turned their heads to take in the enormous man stalking awkwardly towards the door in the ice rink wall. I had to hand it to Blake, though: as opposed to our last experience on the bus, today he took his environment's reaction with good humour, probably due to his excitement at the prospect of a different kind of exercise. What an admirable attitude – back when I still used mirrors on a daily basis, I had always been conscious about every hair out of its place. I could tell how tense Blake was when he placed his first foot on the ice but when he pulled the other one in and immediately began to glide a few feet, he exhaled sharply and shifted again to propel himself forward.

If 'Watching a super obese man ice-skate' isn't on your bucket list, you need to put it there immediately because Blake skating was a sight to behold. His thick thighs shifting under his impossibly wide rear, propelling his massive body forward while his bulging arms provided the necessary counter-motion reduced my panties to a pool of slick wetness instantly. It was a mouth and nether-region watering spectacle and my feet glided across the ice behind him with a will of their own in order not to miss a beat.

In my early twenties, I had once briefly attempted to research my body's inexplicable reaction but had quickly closed the internet browser with a prickling face and hoped whatever organization was creating a user profile on me would chalk it up to general research. Yes, that's how paranoid I used to be. My physical response to Blake's striptease, however, had roused what had lain dormant for so long and ultimately caused me to engage in more research before I had recorded my latest YouTube video.

A few search terms had quickly led me through articles, forums and videos, and judging by the state of my underwear after only twenty minutes I had my answer. I was an FFA, a Female Fat Admirer. The more I read about like-minded women discovering, coming to terms and ultimately embracing their predilections, the more I felt a weight lift off my shoulders, or more aptly put, a closet door open. Although I wasn't quite ready yet to push it open all the way, I felt certain that my body would take care of outing myself sooner or later. I knew now what I wanted and that nothing less would ever do. Blake needed to lose weight urgently, no doubt about that, and I would support him for as long as he let me, but that didn't mean he wasn't attractive to me at his current size.

After two more rounds that reminded me to use a panty liner next time, Blake glided over to the wall where I joined him a moment later. Although he was breathing heavily, his face was almost split in two by his radiant smile, and my hands were itching with the urge to hug him close.

"You're doing great!" I beamed at him instead with both thumbs up.

"The last… time I did this was… probably 200 lbs. ago," he panted back, resting his forearms heavily on the wall, "but I haven't had… this much fun… in years."

It took him a while to control his breathing and to straighten up again but when he did, he reached out to pull me close. "Thank you."

I didn't respond. There was no need to.

We agreed to skate individually for a while, each in our own rhythm, and I began to dart over the surface as quickly as I dared, over time even in close proximity to our few fellow skaters, some of whom moved with admirable skill despite their age. Nonetheless I never quite lost sight of the largest figure on the ice who was making increasingly faster progress.

The large digital clock informed me we had been skating for thirty minutes when I joined Blake at last. "Want to skate together for a bit?" I smiled at him, taking care not to let my eyes wander over his by now jacketless body too obviously.

"I thought you'd never ask."

For a while we glided side by side, gradually picking up speed before I noticed Blake was tiring. As much as the ice enabled even an obese man to glide with relative ease, his large body has unaccustomed to prolonged exercise.

"Coffee break?" I suggested with a nod at the door to the small cafeteria and was met with a grateful nod. "The last one at the door has to treat!" I threw at him, waited until he nodded and sped off.

A quick check over my shoulder informed me that Blake was quickly falling behind; what it also did, however, was to mess with my precarious anatomical arrangement on the slippery surface. Before I knew what had happened, I was sitting flat on my butt, the sound of my companion's deep laughter echoing in my ears. Again, I had never dealt well with humour at my own expense but at this moment, I joined in Blake's laughter readily, only to close my mouth again a moment later. Every movement, even the act of laughing, caused my tailbone to communicate its displeasure, and the cold wetness didn't exactly help either.

"Well," Blake's voice drifted down to me, "first of all, thank you for treating, second: are you OK?"

"Mostly," I grimaced up into his grinning face and availed myself of his outstretched hands, carefully pulling myself to my feet again. Due to his considerable anatomy, I couldn't help but brush along his beckoning midriff, temporarily alleviating the painful throb.

"How's your butt?"

I couldn't resist. Slightly turning to offer him visual access to my rear assets, I made a show of glancing over my shoulder and probing my cheeks with both hands before I turned back to him to announce my verdict: "Perfect of course."

Blake's previously concerned expression eased into a sly smile as he followed my hands' progress. "Can't say I disagree."

To this day I can't say who initiated it but all of a sudden, I found myself engulfed by the pliable warmth and tasted that indescribable taste of someone your body has approved of long before your mind has had a chance to catch up. Everywhere around me, there was softness. Homecoming, shelter, but also tingles and the acute need to press skin to skin.

"Hey, young man, careful with that skinny lady of yours!"

Abruptly both of our heads whipped around to the petite white-haired gentleman in the bright green jacket who had just sped by and turned over his shoulder again to grin at us. Although neither his tone nor face conveyed disgust or derision, I jerked away from Blake as if the curse had returned for him. I caught a glimpse of his falling face before my eyes dropped to my skates.

"Uh-huh, how about we get coffee another time?" his low voice drifted down to me eventually. "You hurt yourself, we should get out of here."

"Do you mind? The pain *is* getting worse and my butt is wet."

I could have pounded my forehead on the ice the instant the words left my mouth. Blake wasn't an idiot; he knew that was not the main reason for my reaction. Whatever progress I had deluded myself into having made during our last bus ride, to be labelled a morbidly obese man's girlfriend had catapulted me back into my old gutless ways, no matter how much I had enjoyed our kiss.

The silence between us, while we waited for and at last entered the bus home, seemed to weigh as much as Blake, and he kept not only his eyes firmly averted from mine but also his thighs as far as he managed to on the three seats we occupied together. I could feel our fellow riders' stares boring into us but they were not what caused my face to prickle and my head to pound. Whereas Blake had listened, stroked and comforted me through my pain, I had let him down, just like his ex. From what I had gathered, she had been so ashamed of him in the end that she probably didn't even want to be seen with him anymore. Nobody deserved that, in particularly not since I felt truly attracted to him. Treating myself to a much-needed inhale, I willed my swirling thoughts to focus: did I want something to happen between us?

Well, duh.

OK then. Did I want *more* than that to happen between us? A long sigh escaped me as my elbows sank into my thighs and my head into my hands. As much as I had sought to keep him at arm's length initially, all the better had I gotten to know him over the past few days, and every day I liked more what I discovered, inside and out. It wasn't the fact that I could touch him or that I felt lonely, it was *him* I wanted by my side. There was no way to tell whether we were compatible in the long run but then again who knew ever when they met someone new?

What was it that was holding me back then? What could be more personal than physical, emotional and character preferences in a partner, so how insane would I have to be to keep searching for a socially approvable one? Heck, bowing to public opinion was what had earned me my bad karma and ultimately landed me in my current predicament! There, I had my answer.

That left Blake's side of the story. He was a single heterosexual male, which meant he at least entertained sexual fantasies about me. However, with my body type differing so far from his ex's, what were the chances that he found me attractive enough as a partner? Where overweight guys had once hardly dared to make eye contact with me, here I was doubting my own lack of attraction in the eyes of a super morbidly obese man – did it get any more ironic than that?

Yet I had to try. Slowly I straightened, catching Blake's troubled gaze darting between me as well as two teenagers with their smartphones not so subtly tilted in our direction. If there ever was a right moment to declare my intentions, at least non-verbally, it was now, despite the very likely risk that mine was not a body type compatible with Blake's preferences. After another deep inhale I fixed my eyes firmly on his face until he turned to me. Next, I scooted forward and gently but firmly pulled at his heavy hand until it dropped onto what was left of the seat cushion behind me. *Please, Blake*, I willed him to understand, *let me make up for what I did.*

Whether it was my gaze boring into his or the teenagers' giggles, at last, he lifted his arm and settled it around my shoulders as far as possible while I scooted back into his softness with a barely suppressed sigh of relief and pleasure. One of the two boys lowered his phone, his jaw slightly unhinged as he took in the scene before his bespectacled eyes, and I couldn't resist puckering up my lips at him before I pulled Blake's heavy arm closer around me and rested my left hand on his plush thigh. However, the elderly skater's comment had spooked me earlier, declaring myself this huge man's at least temporarily significant other came naturally once I handed over the reins to my heart and body.

Not one word was exchanged until we exited the bus twenty minutes later, nor when I resolved the predicament of our arms awkwardly dangling between us by slipping my hand in his. Only when we began to tackle the incline and Blake's breathing and manner of motion revealed his exhaustion, undoubtedly fueled by our previous skating exercise, did I disengage my hand from his so he could use his arms to propel himself forward as I had watched him do several times before.

"E- Ela?"

Half an hour had passed since I had looked into his face last, and since then large amounts of colour and transpiration had added to it.

"You... can go ahead, I will... catch up with you," he panted, whilst his massive chest heaving, and in the way, I had been able to relate to his needs from the beginning, I sensed he wasn't offering but asking, so I only nodded, brushed my hand along his arm and trudged up the path alone. By the time a glistening and splotchy-cheeked Blake dragged himself inside the house, I was just finishing up my preparations for a potato soup, so I only greeted him over my shoulder and let him get rid of his clothes in semi-privacy.

"Coffee?" I inquired at last with another smile over my shoulder.

"Definitely. I… I just need to wash up a little first."

He joined me at the kitchen counter ten minutes later, wearing a fresh T-shirt and droplets in his hair, and I kept my eyes on his with difficulty as I handed him a mug, grazing my fingers along his. Watching Blake's waddling gait shift his masses under the fabric was quickly turning into an addiction and I felt my breathing deepen as my eyes invariably strayed over what they had been secretly feasting on all day. The motion of his setting down the mug on the counter caused my eyes to dart upwards again and my hands to abandon their drinking utensil as well.

As opposed to our kiss on the ice earlier, this time I knew exactly that it was I who reached out to pull him close for another toe-curling kiss. His response was instant, and suddenly there was softness all around me again, a softness I set out to explore with greedy fingers before his followed suit a moment later. When Blake's bulk backed me against the kitchen counter, I swiftly hoisted myself up and spread my legs to let his abundant mass nestle between us before I slipped my fingers underneath the hem of his T-shirt. Although Blake released a sharp gasp, his ensuing breathing bespoke his eagerness for my touch, and a second later I felt his warm hands roam over my exposed waist as well.

"Couch," I managed to pant in between kisses and wiggled against him until he backed away so I could hop off, dart over to the couch and unfold it before I turned to the delicious man behind me and tugged his T-shirt upwards.

"Ela, wait, I— "

"Do you want this?"

"Y- yes."

"Then shut up."

And with another kiss, I made sure he did. After all, what was the point of hiding? I had seen all of this before and not only knew what lay beneath but I also needed it desperately. After I had rid him of his T-shirt, I sent my sweater, top and bra flying before I dove face first into the beckoning mass of blubber. At some point I had to come up for air but kept my hands where they belonged, kneading and lifting as much as I could fit in my hands.

"Uh—"

"Please let me," I implored the red-cheeked face in front of me, "you once asked me if I wanted to get to know you. I do. This is me getting to know you."

A chuckle emerged from behind Blake's lips. "Can't you get to know my hair instead?"

"Not that you don't have great hair but I want to get to know all of you. Try to relax, you have nothing to worry about."

Although his eyes remained on mine, no sound emerged. Deliberately I let my gaze wander over his exposed torso, nodding in appreciation, a gesture born as much out of conviction as the need to reassure. At last, he answered with a nod and a wobbly smile of his own, which I rewarded with a gentle kiss before I peeled off my jeans to reveal my dark green silk panties. Thank goodness for my karma-induced fondness for high-quality materials, and thank goodness for testosterone as well. Apparently, Blake's body has just decided that it would take what I was offering even though its owner wasn't quite there yet.

"You… you look so beautiful."

"So do you."

Before he could open his mouth to argue, I distracted him with a way more enjoyable alternative and a moment later his hands cupped around my face while his lips provided some of the best kissings I had ever experienced. He didn't even fight me when I slipped my hands underneath the elastic waistband of his jeans and laid bare the bulging mass that was his rear end. Since his thighs were too thick for the jeans to simply drop to his ankles, I carefully nudged him back towards the couch so he would sit and I could fully unwrap the delectable package in front of me.

"Wait. What about…"

The almost panicky note in Blake's voice caused the haze of lust to fade abruptly. Then the realization set in. "Protection?"

I dropped onto the couch next to Blake and let myself fall on my back, glaring at the ceiling. "Son of a bitch. Uh-uh, I didn't mean you."

Chuckling, Blake leaned on his left elbow and bent over me to brush my hair off my face, a motion which caused his blubbery belly to partly slosh on top of me, a promising taste of what was to come. And come it would! I pushed myself up and onto my feet again and hurried back into my clothes.

"What are you doing?"

"Heading into town to get the biggest box of condoms there is."

When I turned, I was holding a dubious but increasingly sly grin. He finally understood that I meant business.

"Don't you dare take the edge off while I'm gone. I want you so horny you can't see straight."

CHAPTER FIFTEEN
Blake: World end

Ela's goodbye kiss still lingered on my lips as I laid back on the couch. 'That you can't see straight'. Funny she would say that to me. The way she'd been pawing my fat body, it seemed *she* was the one who couldn't see straight. Now I could only hope that the twenty-five minutes or so she'd be gone wouldn't cool her off and make her change her mind.

A knock on the door suddenly yanked me back into reality. Who could that be? Hastily I pulled my T-shirt back on and my pants up before crossing over to the door.

"Who is it?"

"The new neighbour."

Neighbour? That didn't bode well for Ela, no matter how friendly the man had sounded. Slowly I opened the door to an Asian man as tall and skinny as Ela. His age was impossible to guess, anything from sixteen to forty. A good-looking guy if you were into Asian. Uh, I didn't mean for that to sound racist. His eyes behind the frameless glasses bulged as he took in all of me but he rallied quickly and held out his hand.

"Uh, hello there, my name is Nguyen Truong Anh, but you can call me Max. Are you the owner of this house?"

Huh? First accent-free German, then a bunch of Asian syllables and now 'Max'? Automatically, though, I shook the guy's hand, instantly liking him despite the threat he posed as a 'neighbour'. Was he going to build a house here then? I'd thought none of the properties was for sale.

"Blake. Uh, no, I'm not, my…" what was Ela to me? Oh, what the heck, I wasn't going to explain our relationship to a stranger. "My girlfriend is. She isn't around at the moment, though."

The man's eyes widened for a moment but then he smiled. "Well, I'm glad to meet *you* then. I just came by to introduce myself and to say sorry in advance for all the construction that will be going on over the next months. My aunt, uncle and I are having the old restaurant building torn down and rebuilt from scratch. It's going to be amazing, have you ever had Vietnamese or Khmer cuisine?"

"Khmer?"

"Cambodian."

"Uh, no, can't say I have."

"You must come when everything is ready then. We'll even give you a neighbour discount," he added with a wink. "I might be back with more bad news, such as noise or obstructions you must expect, but the real work isn't starting until the danger of frost is over."

"Uh, alright, thanks for letting us know."

"Sure thing. Sorry, got to go, just wanted to say hi. And Bye."

"Bye."

Then the guy jogged back along the gravel path to the main road. As if on auto-pilot, I trudged over to the couch again and fell back, letting the news sink in. Whether Ela would change her mind about sex with me while she was gone was the least of my worries now. A new restaurant and therefore a steady stream of people if the business went well meant that Ela's carefully built world was coming to an end. What was she going to do? There was no question how she would take the news. Was there a solution, a way to soften the blow for her?

By the time I heard her key in the door, I was still lying there with an arm over my eyes, having come up with exactly nothing. I had just struggled into a sitting position when she stepped in with a mischievous smile and her gloved hand curled around a box of promising size.

"Hey there, look, I got enough to last us for a while." Next, she pulled a giant tube of lube out of her coat pocket before she hurried out of her coat and boots. For once she didn't put them into their assigned places but left the boots in the entry and her coat on the kitchen table, which for her was as good as flinging them left and right. Then she actually did fling her jeans and sweater left and right before she turned around to me. Her eagerness died away at once.

"What's wrong?"

"Nothing." I couldn't tell her now. I needed to think it through how I was going to break the news to her. "Just processing. It's all happening pretty fast."

"Actually," she climbed onto my lap as best as she could manage, "it was about time something happened. We're both shamefully overdue."

And she planted her lips back on mine. For a second I berated myself that I really should tell her but… well, I *was* shamefully overdue, and here I had this scalding hot girl in mouth-watering underwear on my lap. No-brainer.

"Blake? I can't wait any longer."

"Neither can I."

Even though I'd never done it at my current size, I knew which positions worked, and if I hadn't grossed her out until now, she wouldn't object to my belly resting on her back while I entered her from behind. At any rate, it beat laying her down at the edge of the bed with me standing up and burying her under my gut.

As it turned out, my worries were unwarranted. If Ela wasn't a master faker, I made her come in record time. Good thing, too, since I didn't last long either. In fact, hearing her moan the way she did when I entered her almost made me come on the spot. Afterwards, we lay there drenched, she mostly in my sweat. Almost instantly, her hands were back on my body, grabbing and kneading handfuls. She was like a kid at a petting zoo.

"Sorry, is this OK for you?" Her apologetic eyes met mine across the ocean of flesh her hands had disappeared in.

"If it is OK for *you*."

"I keep repeating myself: more than OK."

Why did she keep saying that, and with a smile, too? Coupled with that 'heavy guys' bit from her video, that could actually be interpreted as her being... into me? Of course, there were plenty of skinny FFAs but Ela had admitted to putting down people she thought beneath her, and there was no doubt I fell into that category. There could be no other explanation for her behaviour other than the fact that she was lonely and I was available, although, I would never have thought those two things to be so powerful that she would not only touch but have sex with what Silke had refused to touch.

"Blake?" a pink-cheeked Ela put an abrupt stop to my inner debate, her hands kneading my body with an increasing urgency now, "can you... I mean, would you...?"

"... like to go again?" I finished softly when a blush crept into her cheeks, which deepened when she nodded.

"Yes. If not, I can—"

"Shush," I silenced her by brushing my thumb gently across her full lips. "Yeah, I'd be up for another round."

"Good. Can I... can I be on top this time?"

Wow. It's like I didn't know the woman at all that I had lived with for three and a half weeks. How many sides could one person have? At any rate, I intended to explore all of them as long as she let me. Wordlessly I stuffed some pillows under my lower back so that my belly sloshed towards me a bit and she could seat herself better. I could have felt embarrassed that she had to lift that large apron of fat to find what she was searching for but looking at her I just couldn't. She wanted me just as much as I wanted her, and that was all that counted.

After our amazing second time, even that woman with her never-still hands was exhausted and I held her close against me while I felt her breathing deepen and her beautiful body relax. Later that day – I had drifted off, too – Ela was the first to take a shower. It was as if we both sensed we were not ready to take one together yet if there even was a 'yet'. While Ela was in the bathroom, I changed the bedding, causing her to smile widely and hug me with another deep kiss when she saw the neat couch.

"Your turn," she murmured, gently squeezing the largest roll bulging over the waistband of my sweats while she leaned into another drawn-out kiss. Her time alone in the bathroom clearly hadn't given her any regrets about what we had done. Still, I reflected as I stepped into the shower, it couldn't possibly have meant more to her than sex. Ela might not belong to those people who believed fat equalled ugly, but there were many kinds of fat and I was hardly the attractive kind. Silke was a big girl but she was in great shape, a good dresser and always groomed. Me, on the other hand…

Skinny people have no idea of what it takes to keep several square feet and countless skin folds clean and dry. As I scrubbed my armpits around the bulks of flab, I had to face the facts: I could take care of myself as much as I wanted to but there wasn't much I could do to make myself attractive. I'd gained weight so quickly over the past year that my body had become doughy and saggy. No matter how many pounds I dropped, only a skin-removal surgery would get me back into shape. As for dressing well, the best thing that could be said about my clothes these days was that they covered everything and weren't too snug. It was no wonder Silke had become more and more ashamed of me. Was Ela? She had certainly looked it on the ice rink but then she'd snuggled close to me on the bus, marking me as hers for everyone to see. I just couldn't make sense of her. The best I could hope for was patience and acceptance but probably never attraction. The chances of stumbling across another FFA directly after Silke were simply too minute.

And that was not the only question here. Assuming this thing between us was more than sex and we did become a couple, where would we live? We couldn't stay in this small house but Ela would only be willing to move if her curse/bad karma lifted. That, or if the stream of restaurant patrons would become too much for her, but that was yet another problem to be solved. How, and in particular when would I break the news to her?

When we were lying on the couch again together twenty minutes later and her hands had slipped under my fresh T-shirt again, I couldn't hold back anymore:

"Uh-huh, Ela? The old restaurant down the road, what kind of cuisine was it?"

"Ethiopian," she murmured while her fingers were doing the kind of things on my chest that made you forget whatever thoughts or words you had lined up.

"I… I've never had Ethiopian food," I managed to get out when she pinched my left moob.

"Neither have the Ethiopians."

Abruptly her hands withdrew and her white face came up with both hands clapped over her mouth. "Oh my gosh, that was a terrible thing to say!"

"On the contrary," I chuckled at her while I peeled her fingers off her mouth in order to claim it, "that was a hilarious thing to say. Relax, I'm sure Karma won't decide on an extension." I kissed her. "See?" I kissed her again, feeling her return it this time. "I love your humour. In fact, I love everything I'm discovering about you lately."

Her smile didn't look entirely convinced but she relaxed enough for me to pull her against me and to place her hands under my T-shirt again.

"But seriously," she began again while tracing one of my many creases, "I don't know what kind of restaurant it was. They were already closed when I moved here. Why do you ask?"

"No reason. Just wondering who would open up a business out here." I just couldn't ruin the moment.

"Well, as you can see, it was a bad idea. Lucky for me," she smirked and snuggled closer. The terrible secret I carried with me suddenly seemed to weigh more than even I did.

As I had for the past few days, I woke up to the scent of Ela, but the pair of eager hands under my T-shirt was a new addition. I still couldn't believe we had slept together, although judging by the motion underneath the duvet I was about to get another piece of proof. Indeed a few minutes later we were both panting hard and slick with sweat again. At that rate, we would go through a set of bed sheets every day but Ela seemed as if she couldn't care less.

All throughout the breakfast preparations, she kept brushing, patting or pressing kisses on my skin in passing, but as much as I would have liked to lose myself in the feeling, the Asian-restaurant matter increasingly bore down on me.

My preoccupation wasn't lost to an observant person like Ela.

"Blake, what's wrong?" she finally laid her hand over mine on the breakfast table, forcing me to look at her.

"I..." God, how was I going to say this?

"Do you… I mean, should we not have—"

"No!" Instantly I grabbed her right hand with both of mine. "I don't regret a second, do you hear me? It's… it's something else."

"Blake, you're freaking me out," she prodded when I swallowed but no sound came out.

Another gulp and then, bit by bit, the events from the day before tumbled out. I would never have suspected a Snow-white lookalike could pale even more, but she did, at least until her arms shot out and shoved me hard.

"You bastard, you waited until I'd slept with you to tell me that?!"

While her hands had sunk too deep into my blubber to inflict actual damage, she was now on her feet and pummeling her fists into my right upper arm. I barely managed to push myself to my feet under her pelting punches but at last, succeeded in throwing my arms around her and keeping them by her side.

"Let go of me, you jerk! Leave me alone, just leave me alone!"

As strong as she was, she was no match against me, of course, and after some more useless struggling, she suddenly broke down crying and slumped in my arms like a deflated balloon. It was as if all life had suddenly gone out of her and she clung to me while she sobbed as hard as she had done after the failed grocery-store experiment. It was so unfair. Even if she had been as shallow and mean as she had insisted, nobody deserved what she had to go through. I mean, how much suffering could one person take, even one as strong as Ela?

At last, the earthquake of sobs abated and the battered beautiful woman in my arms went still. Only for a moment, though. I could practically feel the cogs turning in her admirable head.

"There has to be something I can do to stop the construction."

I couldn't help it, a small chuckle escaped me at that. "Short of monkey-wrenching or contaminating the ground, I don't see how."

I ran my fingers through her hair, massaging her scalp and finally moved down to her chin, turning her face gently up to mine.

"Ela, you have to face it: things are changing. Construction crews and machinery are going to invade your space and then the patrons of the restaurant will take over. Life as you have built and known it is over. And perhaps that's a good thing," I added when I saw her eyebrows contract and her mouth open.

"How can that be a good thing?"

"Because you weren't living when we met. You were existing. One more year on your own and I think you would have fallen apart." Her first YouTube video had made that all too clear.

"What's the alternative?" she threw at me, struggling out of my arms, "move to Oman?"

"Not a bad idea," I grinned at her before I sobered. "But how about if you try rejoining German society first?"

"No way. You were there at the store; my karma is still bad."

"Again," I raised both palms, "it didn't work with that one guy but maybe it will with other people. But that's not what I'm getting at: I think you should try how you can live among people again, no matter if you can touch them or not. For instance, I'd really like introduce you to my friends Lars and Evelyn – the ones I visited a while ago – and make you see what it feels like to be in good company. And they are. They would respect your personal space and not pester you with questions. I mean, you'd have to give them some explanation why you're keeping your distance, trauma for instance or a skin condition, but they'd respect that. Those two are amazing and I'm positive they'd like you, too."

I could practically her mind race. Meeting my friends would come with great risks for both them and her. Then again, she knew I was right: she had been existing, not living. My entering her lonely, silent world had shown her how much she needed the presence of other people.

At last looked back at me. "Do they have any pets or kids? I can come up with some sort of explanation to adults but a child or animal might hurl itself on me unasked."

"No, they have neither but… Evelyn is pregnant."

"The clock is ticking then."

I hated to agree with her but it was a fact. At last, she nodded. "Alright."

"I'm proud of you." She let herself be pulled into a hug. "And I'm really sorry I didn't tell you right away. The whole time since yesterday I tried to think of the best way to break the news to you, but then you came home all smiling and with this huge box of condoms…"

Her giggle caused me to release my hold on her and face her. "I didn't know if I would have another chance with you, so I took this one. It was low, I know."

"It's OK. And I'm sorry for lashing out at you. You were only the messenger."

"Don't worry about it."

Then her arms tightened around me again and I felt her lips on my neck. It was settled then, I would introduce her to Lars and Eve. The million-euro question was, though: as what would I introduce her?

CHAPTER SIXTEEN

Ela: Opening

"You drive like an old lady."

I gunned down the cheerful face in the rear-view mirror. "Given you're the most useless passenger ever, I don't see why you should be entitled to an opinion."

That made Blake grin even more broadly. "I'm not a passenger."

"Useless cargo then."

He snickered and I let myself join in. Since I wasn't hurting Blake with my words, surely, I could crack such jokes without accumulating more bad karma, right? At least he took the transportation arrangements in good humour since we had decided to drive due to the pelting rain and the considerable distance from the bus station to Lars and Evelyn's house. Humour, however, was the furthest thing from my mind. What if some uptight law-abiding neighbour would alert the police that I was transporting a person in the back of my van? Also, the psychological-trauma excuse I had permitted Blake to convey to his friends as a heads-up sounded plausible in theory, but what if something happened that caused them to touch me after all?

I simply had to believe I could pull this off today. Perhaps then there was a chance for me to rejoin society, which was what I had hoped for ever since I moved here, only I had grown too comfortable with my sheltered existence. I had to try, and as fate or Karma would have it, I had someone by my side to help me.

However, what if Blake's friends asked if we were together? As far as I was concerned, I knew what I wanted. With each new bed-sheet encounter I couldn't believe it had taken me so long to face the facts. How many others were out there who weren't even aware they were into big people because it was so counter-cultural? How many who never questioned their choice in skinny partners while secretly wondering why they couldn't get excited about their bodies? And there was Blake as a person: this strong, witty, passionate and tenacious man I just couldn't picture my life without anymore. Bottom line, I was his for the taking, but would he *want* to take me?

At last, I pulled up to the curb of the last house on the left. Around a dozen two-story homes from the 1930s with a sandstone base and old-fashioned roofing tiles lined this part of the long street that eventually widened and lead through fields to another, more rural part of town.

By the time we approached the wide sandstone steps, a lanky brunette our age with thinning hair had appeared in the doorway next to a short, curvy woman with a honey-coloured bob and a bulging baby belly. Blake hugged the man first before his wide grin morphed into a gentle smile and he embraced the short woman carefully.

"You look terrific!" she beamed up at him, running her eyes all over his body, "it is so good to see you again."

No, I did not count down the seconds until the woman's body and eyes finally unfastened themselves from Blake's. I didn't. OK, fine, it was six.

"Guys, this is Ela," Blake now smiled at me and pulled me close in a gentle, one-armed hug.

"Hey."

The couple's genuine smile and the fact that they kept their hands to themselves brought my blood pressure down to a reasonable value, and it was with a lighter heart that I followed them into the kitchen where whole-wheat pasta with a promising-smelling sauce awaited gustatory recognition. Despite the modern appliances, the couple had preserved the historic flair of the kitchen, and the broad scuffed bench offered a secure and comfortable seat even to Blake's wide bottom, which I couldn't help but watch spread in appreciation.

Thankfully the men availed themselves of the conversational oars at once, with Evelyn occasionally adding her own small paddle, while I contented myself with floating and bobbing along. Clearly, Blake had asked his friends to stay away from personal topics in order to ease me back into the company of people. My hero.

When the conversation turned to computers, well, actually to Lars teasing Blake about being a computer illiterate, I couldn't help but hurry to his defence, and soon he and his wife managed to coax more information out of me than I had initially planned to volunteer. I also noticed Evelyn's eyes commuting increasingly between Blake and me. Although I had honed my skill of emotional concealment over the years, the novel sensation of tingles at the sight of Blake's shifting body mass apparently infused my face with sufficient colour for an observant person to deduce their origin.

"Are you guys ready for dessert yet?" Evelyn asked at some point, "fruit salad," she added with a meaningful look at Blake, causing his cheeks to comment instantly.

"I'd say we let this settle for a while, Eve," Lars patted his minuscule paunch, "and in the meantime, Blake could take a look at that rust spot under the rear window you mentioned."

"I'd love to, but let's help clear the table first, OK?"

The look the couple exchanged at Blake's comment spoke volumes and explained why he hadn't turned to them for help despite the available space in their home. Clearly, his erstwhile nonexistent cleanliness would have put a too severe strain on their friendship.

"Are you a car person, too, Ela," Evelyn put in while Blake hefted himself to his feet, "or would you like a tour of the house in the meantime?"

I barely caught Blake's encouraging smile, my mind already tangled in the ramifications of Evelyn's seemingly innocuous suggestion. Exposing myself to the grilling she was about to unleash on me without Blake's protective presence? Then again, I had come here today to test how I functioned among people.

"Sure," I replied at last and rose, my eyes conveying to Blake it was OK for him to go ahead. Evelyn motioned to me to enter the rooms on the first floor before her, each one equipped with original hardwood floors and high ceilings. The slightly crooked stairs in the same wood, well-worn in the middle and smooth from where generations of hands had polished the bannister were what drew my eye especially, and I wished I could have sat down on them for a while and run my hands over the historic wood.

"You have a soft spot for old houses, don't you?"

Evelyn smiled at me when we had reached the upper level, a little breathless from the exertion of carrying a tiny extra person up the stairs.

"I didn't use to think so but I guess I do. Uh, shall we sit for a while?"

"That would be good, thank you," she chuckled, leading us on towards the bedroom where she gratefully sank down on the metal double bed. "Goodness, that feels so much better. Sometimes this little guy – or girl – feels as heavy as a beer keg. Honestly, hats off to Blake for getting around as well as he does."

Naturally, my cheeks turned into a white-hot inferno at my companion's innocuous comment and I braced myself on the bedspread, bending forward so my hair would shield my face.

"You know; I think it's incredible that you took Blake in. Not just put him up for one night but letting him stay. We both know he isn't easy to live with."

At last, I dared to turn to her, finding that her eyes were resting on me in warm curiosity. "Neither am I," I grimaced at her, "I'm sure he gave you an earful about how much I was on his case in the beginning."

"I'll admit he did but he does need a kick in his big butt on a regular basis. Seriously, you're good for him. I've never seen him look so well."

"Uh, Evelyn, Blake and I are not together." At least as far as I knew. "Besides, I thought he and his ex-were perfect for each other."

Evelyn tilted her head. "In a way," she began after a moment, "but his weight problem started when he met her. I mean, he has always been a big guy but Silke… she preferred him even bigger." I chose not to comment on that and hopefully my face didn't either. Where Blake was concerned, it never checked back with me. "Anyway, in the beginning, I was glad for Blake that she didn't try to put him on a diet but then it turned out she happily watched him pile on pound after pound instead." Her face suddenly looked as if its owner was undergoing an extended lemon-tasting experience. "Well, until it got too much even for her and she dropped him."

From what I had gathered about Blake's ex, she appeared to be a kind, loving person, yet the little black – or green – part of me couldn't help but rejoice in Evelyn's low opinion of her. Had Blake meanwhile come to the same conclusion or was he still planning to win Silke back? While I had surrendered to him heart and body, to him it might have been just sex.

Evelyn, meanwhile, had regained her cheerful countenance. "Silke never had him in hand as you do. I couldn't believe it when he took off his shoes and cleared the table unasked, also the last time he visited."

A grin tugged at my mouth at the memory of our first fight. "It took a lot of hard work, and hard words. Initially, I thought him about as trainable as a cat."

Evelyn laughed, moving as if to nudge me but quickly pulled back when I flinched.

"Sorry." After a protracted period of tense silence, Evelyn drew breath. "Ela? Whatever it is, you don't have to be ashamed of it or feel pressured to explain yourself. I'm just glad Blake managed to convince you to come, and I hope we'll see you again."

"Thanks."

"And who knows, maybe you'll change your mind someday about you two just being friends. I know he's a lot to look at right now but he's a keeper."

My thoughts exactly, although I would deem 'and' the more appropriate conjunction rather than 'but'. His size was part of his being a keeper – not his current, unhealthy size but his tendency to be heavy. I refused to revert back to shame for my newly discovered preferences, but after hearing about Silke's part in Blake's condition, how could I ever tell him I was attracted to his figure? Wasn't that a guarantee for his abandoning his diet sooner or later?

"Sorry, hon," a sigh to my right pierced through the swirling mist of my reflections, "I need to use the bathroom. Junior is using my bladder as a trampoline again. Uh, are you ready for dessert yet?"

"Sounds good."

"Would you get the guys?"

"Sure."

Minuscule snowflakes were lazily drifting down onto the fabric of my coat as I hurried towards the narrow garage attached to the right of the house. Despite the biting cold, the men had left the corrugated-metal door slightly ajar.

"So, you and Ela, huh?"

I knew I should make my presence known but who wouldn't pause to eavesdrop when they heard their name?

"Geez, what did I tell you fifteen minutes ago?"

"I don't remember," Lars declared with an audible grin.

"That I didn't know and didn't want to talk about it."

"I think you do know. You and I both know, as does Eve."

"It's not that simple! Even if she feels the same way, I can't take her at face value."

"What do you mean? She seems pretty straight-forward to me."

Ditto! Except for the omission of my preference for his size, I had never lied to Blake.

"She… she's dealing with some pretty tough shit and for some reason, I'm the only one she can open up to."

I had to hand it to him, phrased like that I sounded almost normal.

"Whatever she may feel towards me, it's just be-cause she's feeling vulnerable. Plus, we're cooped up at her place pretty much 24/7, so it was only a matter of time before something happened."

"Aha, so you did close the deal!"

"Seriously, cut it out, Lars! It doesn't mean any-thing. We'd never work out in real life. And now please just let it go, OK?"

I'd heard enough, especially the 'It doesn't mean anything' part. Blake was doing a good deed for the sex-deprived curse, a deed that got him some much-needed action in bed as long as he was still too big to be with someone normal. Automatically I felt my sense of preservation engage. I needed to make it through this afternoon, and once home, I would break the news to Blake: he had to leave. Every time I laid eyes on him, it would remind me of what he saw in me and that he would fade from my life eventually.

Perhaps he even had a point about our unusual circumstances and enforced proximity being responsible for our attraction to one another. While I would never again doubt my appreciation for his body type, I might be deluding myself about my feelings for him as a person. After all, we still hardly knew one another. The worst part, however, was that even if my feelings were true and Blake reciprocated, my preference for his size would ruin his health in the long run. Once I confided in him, there would be no reason for him to follow his diet anymore.

After a deep breath and some noise for effect, I poked my head inside the garage and informed the men that dessert was ready, keeping my eyes mostly on Lars. Back in the house I subtly manoeuvred myself next to Evelyn instead of Blake and managed to steer the conversation to any topic but Blake and myself.

Only after the two had, respectively, hugged and waved goodbye to us and we had driven in silence for a while did I catch a hint of concern in the eyes that met mine in the rear-view mirror.

"Ela? Is everything alright?"

"Meeting your friends have given me a lot of food for thought is all."

Although not technically a lie, it was the first time I had chosen to mislead Blake, who now nodded in misplaced understanding before he turned back around. By the time I pulled into the garage, not one word had been exchanged and my little speech was ready. I would sit him down on the couch, explain calmly and—

"Ela?" Blake's voice and hand stopped me in my tracks before I could leave the garage, and a gentle but firm pressure around my wrist forced me to turn and face their author. "Talk to me. I can tell something is wrong." True, everything was wrong. "We agreed we wouldn't hide from each other anymore," he reminded me, taking hold of my other hand, his motion automatically causing his belly to brush against mine.

A deep inhale finally dispelled the shower of tingles and coaxed out my first words. "We need to talk."

"Great, the four words that unleash hell."

"Not hell but the truth," I told my boots, gently disengaging my hands from his before I looked back at him. "Blake, it's time you move on."

When I saw him open his mouth, I pressed on lest he deters me from what every fibre of my being was struggling against in the first place. "Our little world here, it's a bubble. It's not real. What we think we're feeling isn't real. You're doing great with your diet but nobody knows how long *my* condition will last. Maybe it will last forever. If you don't get out soon, each day you'll feel more obligated to stay with me because you're the only one immune and I can't let you do that. You deserve a normal life and a normal partner. You should get out while you can."

Another swallow dislodged more words I wished I didn't have to utter. "You mentioned once that your boss would take you back on whenever you're ready, even at the office until you can work in the shop again. I'd say with your computer skills you stand a good chance now. You can stay here until you have that job and can afford an apartment but it would be best if we stayed out of each other's way until then. We did a pretty good job of that before."

"You've been listening to me and Lars talking, haven't you?" Blake finally demanded when my gaze had dropped to my boots again.

"I didn't mean to but yes. And you were entirely right. What we have isn't real and it wouldn't be fair to keep you here."

"Ela, I thought we had talked about this. We were going to find out if the condition has changed for more people than me. Lars and Eve think you're awesome and I believe there's a good chance you'll be able to touch people that like you and that you like back. Let me do this. You helped me and now I'm helping you."

"But you shouldn't." My eyes dared to fix themselves on his at last. "What if the key is not finding likeable people but helping others? After all, I helped you and could suddenly touch you. If I start taking again instead of giving, Karma will strike with a vengeance."

The force with which Blake expelled his next words could have knocked over a person of my former friend Denise's stature. "It all comes down to karma for you, doesn't it? You don't want me to leave because you're so selfless and want me to have a normal life but because you need a new project, a new challenge and therefore a chance for more good karma!"

He shook his head as mirthless chuckles filled the stillness of the garage. "That's all I ever was to you, a project! Is that the reason you slept with me, besides taking the edge off? Show the fat guy a food time and earn some more good karma?"

"No, it's not like that!"

"It's exactly like that!" he roared, abruptly causing my feet to opt for spatial change. "Don't worry, I'll start packing right away. Now that you've house-trained me, I'm sure Lars and Eve will let me stay and you'll have your perfect fat-free life back."

"This is not about your weight!" At least not only.

"Isn't it? Admit it, Ela: Eve asked you if we were together, didn't she?"

"Some… something to that effect."

"I knew it!" he spat at me, "and now you're panicking just like you did at the ice rink. You're ashamed of being taken for a super fat guy's girlfriend! Using me as your boy toy is fine as long as nobody else knows!"

"No, I…"

"If I'm wrong, then why are you blushing? Why, huh? What aren't you telling me?"

That I'm attracted to the man inside the hottest body I have ever laid eyes, fingers and teeth on, and that I want to be with him! Only I couldn't permit any of these words to even peek out of my mouth, not after what I now knew about Silke's role in Blake's predicament.

With each silent second, his reddened, contorted features sagged like sluggish molasses. "Yeah, thought so," he finally nodded when the last facial muscle had slipped into place, "I'm out."

It took me a while to convince my mental and physical faculties to deal with the situation at hand, and by the time I finally let myself inside the house, Blake was already transferring the contents of his chest of drawers into a big backpack with the same measure of care and gentleness he probably felt like applying to me.

"Blake," I addressed his broad back at last, "please don't leave like this."

"Why not?" he glared over his shoulder, "you want me to leave, so what does it matter if I do it now or in a week?"

"I meant, please don't leave mad. It's not what you're thinking."

The current fistful of voluminous fabric dropped back into the drawer as their owner slowly turned on the spot. "Then what am I supposed to think?"

As opposed to our showdown in the garage, his voice held no trace of judgment, only hopeful curiosity. This was my last chance to come clean and yet I could offer him just as little as a few minutes before.

Until now I never knew with how much con-tempt a man could infuse a nod. A moment later he resumed packing while I stood rooted to the spot, helplessly following the terrible events unfurl.

By the time Blake had shouldered the backpack and turned to me in the open doorway one last time, not one muscle in his usually so readable face stooped to communicate with me. Even if I found the courage to confide in him now, my words would undoubtedly fall on hard, icy ground with no hope of credulity taking root.

"Lars will come for my stuff within the next days. Don't worry," he flashed me a derisive grin, "he will keep your address to yourself, not that you'll live here much longer anyway. Good luck finding your next karma project."

The bang of the door left his words and a few dead leaves scattering in his wide wake.

CHAPTER SEVENTEEN

Ela: Courage

Dead leaves on my impeccable floor. Even when Blake walked out of my life, he did so leaving a mess behind. See, we would never have worked out in the real world. We'd been thrown together by extreme circumstances and that was all there was to it. Truly. Then why could I picture picking him up from work, checking apartment ads and… introducing him to my… my mom? If voices can crack on a word, so can thoughts. It was as if I physically felt something snap.

The next things that slowly penetrated my over-taxed mind were a sodden mattress beneath me and the near impossibility of raising my pounding head, a suitable complement to the sensation in my chest. Creeping despair twisted its fingers around my chest, infusing each breath with a pain I felt would be my constant companion from now on instead of the one that had walked out on me earlier.

I'd never believed I would one day revert to my collegiate habit of dragging myself out of bed feet, knees and rear end first, but somehow, I managed to convey myself back into the other room. What now? 8:20. The mere notion of composing dinner was met by a sulky silence on my stomach's part.

Sweep away the leaves? What for, it was not as if I expected guests anytime soon. Or ever again. Perhaps I could record a video? Nope, I was all out of advice.

A mighty yawn suddenly tore from my throat, painfully stretching skin coated with a layer of dried tears. With my back to the mirror, I slowly dragged an icy cold washcloth across my face until I felt myself shiver from the copious number of drops that had trickled underneath my sweater and joined their dried-up lachrymal cousins. Blindly I turned and reached for the first towel my fingers brushed against.

Oh, God. The instant my nostrils picked up Blake's scent, my knees buckled and I slumped onto the floor, some residual wetness from the shower instantly soaking the bottom of my jeans. With their reservoirs literally drained, my overtaxed eyes only contracted a few times before throwing in the figurative towel. Suddenly a non-figurative one, a green one, slowly came into focus: Blake's. Having accompanied my fall, it was lying next to me in a crumpled heap, almost like in our early days.

No, the image wasn't quite right yet. Gratefully catching a second wind, I heaved myself to my feet and yanked open the mirror cabinet, the force sending a small packet of cotton swabs falling and a few spilling out over the floor. Perfect. Next, I balled up four tissues and sent them flying before I opened the toilet seat and surveyed my handiwork. It was as if he'd be back any moment for me to yell at him for making such a mess.

The hysterical giggle ricocheting off the tiled walls would have done a sorceress proud. One hour without Blake and I was already on my way to insanity.

A new day fluttered its eyelids. I didn't. If mirrors and I ever decided to work through our dysfunctional relationship, a day that arrived with what felt like a Titanic's cargo area worth of suitcases under my eyes was not the right time to start therapy. This was a day meant to be spent in bed. Burying my aching face and bare skin deeper in the plush mass next to me on the couch, I greeted my favourite scent.

No. No, no, no, no! The scent was almost gone and the plushness was all wrong, too. Forcing open my leaden eyelids, at last, I glared at Blake's oversize duvet case I had stuffed with everything I could find the day before and rearranged into the shape I would never forget.

No, off! Out!

All my limbs simultaneously fought off the offending bundle I had hugged close only moments ago. After taking care to kick and stampede over it to punish it properly for its outrageous non-Blakeness, I marched into the bathroom with marginally warmer feelings about this day, only to stop dead in my tracks in the open doorway at the sight of last night's mess.

Have you ever peed, drunk and cried at the same time? It works. Sitting on the toilet, I gulped water from my toothbrush cup, fueling the fresh stream of tears trickling down my cheeks and onto my bare torso. Only when every square inch of my skin featured goosebumps the size of goose eggs, did I drag myself to the bedroom and changed into a hoodie. Next, I watched my hands reach for my coat and my feet slip into my boots before I caught my fingers grab my car keys and my feet trudge over to the van. The folded-up beige blanket in the cargo area still bore the imprint of Blake's literally impressive rear. After having slid the door shut, I lowered myself onto the fabric gently, leaned against the backrests of the driver and passenger seat and hugged my knees close to me.

Just like in the bathroom earlier, the cold that had tiptoed in and wormed its way underneath my clothing caused me to abandon my location, my stiff limbs imparting their discontent instantly. Two mugs of scalding tea later, I was finally ready to contemplate my new existence at last.

Although Blake had only been part of my small world for a month, he had irrevocably altered it. How was I to resume where I had left off when every square foot of this house reminded me that he was no longer part of it? What was the point of carrying on like I had when the construction of the new restaurant was looming on the horizon like Godzilla? Blake was right, my world was coming to an end. I had to follow his advice and try if I could touch other people, and if I couldn't, figure out how to function in normal society anyway.

If I could, I would be able to consider new career paths. The therapist idea resurfaced that had first poked its head in at Blake's question. Perhaps I could work as a diet coach – obviously not for adults given my physical preferences, but perhaps for teenagers. They were particularly prone to eating disorders and should receive help early in their lives, not only through healthy dieting but also through a positive body image. Who would be better suited for that than me? It would mean starting from scratch but I knew I possessed the necessary skill set: resourcefulness, empathy and the ability to bear silences and outrage, just to name a few.

Although each of my thoughts was precariously grounded on the premise that the curse/bad karma would lift, a cluster of giggles escaped from my throat as I rose and spun in a circle with my arms outstretched the way I had done as a kid. A new life. I could do this! And part of my new life would be reaching out to everyone I had left behind in horror and panic, starting with Luciana and her now eight-year-old daughter Emmy. Had her hands fully healed? Did she even remember the incident?

Although I could never explain the truth to my friends, by the time I had composed and sent off the email to an address that hopefully still existed, I felt that my socially acceptable version might actually give her closure. I had written to her that, although I still didn't know what had happened to cause the burns, I had been dealing with severe psychological problems at the time, and seeing her daughter hurt had caused me to snap and run. I hadn't been able to break out of it until recently but now I was starting over and wished to make amends. I hoped she would forgive me. Next, I emailed Denise in similar words, which left only my mom. I would go and meet her, no matter the outcome of the experiment. I would hug her with gloves when necessary and take a risk by explaining the truth.

Something else trailed in the wake of that particular thought. Actually, not 'trailed' as much as 'trudged': Blake. That image that had swum in the lake of my tears yesterday, the one of introducing him to my mother, washed up on shore again. It was because of him that I would see her again and he deserved all the credit for it.

Then again, he deserved, even more, a normal life with a normal partner. Telling Blake how I felt in order to keep him with me would have been nothing but selfish, and my selfishness was what had caused me to end up in my current situation in the first place. If I hoped to start a new phase of my life with my sanity intact, I had to strive to give, not to take.

However, what if I *had* taken? What if Blake felt something for me, too, only I had never let him get a word in edgewise? Had I misconstrued what I had overheard in Lars and Evelyn's garage? Oh God, in that case, I would have hurt him more than I'd ever had before.

I needed to speak to him and make sure, on the chance he would confirm that I had understood him right the first time. However, how could I make sure he would talk to me? If I simply showed up at Lars and Evelyn's house, they might tell me that Blake had asked them not to let me in. Perhaps what had worked with Silke would work with Evelyn, so I sent her a message through my old Facebook account that I hadn't touched in years.

Although it took Evelyn over two hours to respond, it was the answer I had been hoping for, and it was both with a hopeful heart and wobbly knees that I entered the small café close to Evelyn's house she had suggested our meeting. She and a steaming mug were already seated at a corner table, probably unable to insert her baby bump into a booth, and she lifted one small hand in greeting when I entered. Although the thought bordered on blasphemous – or its equivalent for a believer in Karma – at this moment I felt grateful for my condition as it resolved the issue of whether to initiate a hug or not. Therefore, I merely peeled myself out of my coat and scarf, sat and ordered a chai tea from a passing waitress. Whatever a number of words may float out there, for the next few seconds we let them drift past, not even attempting to snag a few downs that would do our situation and relationship justice.

"So, you and Blake?"

So, she was to snag down the very same her husband had used during the conversation I had eavesdropped on.

"I hope so."

"I could tell when you two visited, I just wanted to be sure." The previously neutral face in front of me underwent a subtle but perceptible change for the worse. "Does that mean you can see past his size or that you're into big guys as well?"

Naturally, I felt my cheeks comment before my tongue had a chance to. "The latter, but not in an unhealthy way like his ex," I hurried to add, causing no erosion whatsoever on her critical facade. "I… I like that he is big but I want him to get down to a reasonable weight."

"But you wouldn't mind if there was enough left over?"

"No."

Evelyn's tone expressed her opinion all too clearly but I couldn't and wouldn't deny anymore what had taken me so long to figure out. Meanwhile, I was still being scrutinized like some lab species.

"Does he know?" Evelyn asked at last.

"No. I didn't know myself for sure until recently. And… I'm not sure how he would take the news. I mean, what if that will make him lose his motivation to diet?"

As gradually as before, the features of the woman facing me eased into a new expression, this time one that let me draw hope. Then the head full of short curls shook. "I don't think so, sweetie. The man is crazy about you and will do anything to spend as many healthier years with you as possible. I think you should tell him."

Never before had it taken me so long to utter the two words 'thank you', and rarely had they done so little justice to how I felt.

"Nothing to thank me for," Evelyn smiled back, bracing herself on the small table, most likely to rise and hug me before she bit her lip and lowered herself again. "Sorry."

Only hours before I had resolved I would try, and if there ever was a right moment, this was it.

"Uh-huh, Evelyn? May I try something?"

"Try something? Like what?"

"like touching your hand."

Her eyebrows leapt upwards but after a moment her small hand slid across the smooth surface palm up. After a breath that should have drained the room of oxygen, I slowly reached out with one finger.

There.

Huh, had my fingertip connected with her skin or not? I had to give it another go.

Still no yell, only an expression akin to Blake's when I had done the same with him. I couldn't stop myself, I just had to prod her palm again and again, each new soft stab pulling my cheeks upward. Oh God, it was working, it was working!

"Uh, as glad as I am that you're having fun here, what's going on?"

I could only shake my head, already feeling the tears stream down my cheeks as I shoved my chair back with a screech and pulled the shorter woman to her feet to hug her as much as her baby belly allowed. After a moment I felt her arms around me, too. I could touch her now. There were two people that I could touch, and it was two that I cared about. Was Blake right and that was the pattern?

After a while, Evelyn's beaming face reappeared. "Whatever kept you from touching people before, it looks like you've had a breakthrough."

"With you at least but I'm working on it."

"Come on," she smiled at me, her hands still in mine, "you should come home with me and talk to Blake."

A brief call to Lars verified that both men were not only home but also sitting on the couch together, and since her husband caught on immediately, contenting himself with innocuous 'yepping' and 'noping', Evelyn managed to convey to him that we were coming and Blake was not to be informed.

A few minutes later I entered the house in Evelyn's wake.

"Where is he?" she whispered to her husband who had entered the den to kiss her hello.

The answer to her question stepped into view at this very moment. At the sight of me, his wide arms crossed over his chest, pushing out his belly even more. His thus acquired stance and mien did not bode well for my cause but this was my only shot.

"Hey," my tongue offered before my feet pitched in and stepped closer. "Uh-huh, I need to talk to you."

"You've had your chance."

A few more steps conveyed me to him before he had a chance to fully turn and I managed to turn him halfway back towards me.

"I like big guys!"

If Lars's facial arrangement even remotely resembled Blake's at the moment, they would look really cute in a photo together. However, Lars wasn't who mattered right now. I availed myself of Blake's momentary paralysis in order to grasp both his hands and step in front of him, his belly instantly engaging in contact with me. *Easy, girl, not yet.* I treated myself to another deep breath.

"You asked me before you left what it was that I wasn't telling you. Well, now you know. It just took me some time to admit it to myself and even longer to say it out loud because it totally goes against anything that's normal. Please believe me that I'm not just saying all that because you're the only one that can get close to me."

"Ela, I don't think—"

"Last night I slept on the couch next to a veritable cushion monster I wrapped in anything I could find that smelled like you in order to feel like you were lying next to me. I sat in the back of my van as if it were your lap. Heck, I even left the toilet seat open and made a mess so it would seem you were still there. I miss you, Blake. *You.* I care about you. If you don't feel the same way because I'm admittedly a nutcase, I understand, but I'm working on it. Please give me another chance."

"May I say something?" he asked when the words had stopped rushing out. I only nodded. "Could we take this over to the living room?"

Oh, right. I didn't dare turn my prickling cheeks to Blake's friends but merely followed him into the living room and onto the couch. The dipping motion when he carefully lowered his weight on it did nothing to rein in my lower anatomy's reaction. When Blake turned towards me in his seat, I caught the first glimmer of hope on his round face.

"You're actually serious? You're an FFA? I mean—"

"A female fat admirer, yes."

His eyebrows contracted so sharply they appeared to be kissing. "You know what an FFA is?"

"I only found out recently."

"What… what made you see clearly?" he blurted out, at last, never taking his eyes off mine.

"Looking back, I have always been drawn to bigger men, only I didn't realize it was an attraction that I felt. I only knew my heart wasn't in it when my friends made fun of them, but I went along with the bashing because everyone was doing it and because it made me feel normal." I paused for a moment, mentally apologizing to all the people I had caused so much grief. "Back then I never wanted to look into the issue; I guess deep down I already knew what I would find and I was too scared to face the facts. When you came into my life, though, I couldn't hide what I felt anymore."

After another period of silence, Blake shook his head and his thick fingers ploughed through his hair before he turned back to me. "I can't believe

I'm hearing this. All this time you've never let any-thing on."

"Even when I had finally figured it out, I couldn't tell you because Evelyn said that… that Silke was partly responsible for your weight prob-lem. I thought if you knew how I felt, you'd give up on your diet. I want you so much the way you are but I want even more for you to be healthy."

When his mien darkened and his head turned towards the living-room door, I placed one hand on his wide thigh. "Please don't be mad at her."

After a moment, Blake's contorted features re-laxed a little. "Ela, you're nothing like Silke. I thought we'd stay together through… well," a wry grin stole into his face, "not thick and thin but thick and thicker."

Despite the tension holding my mind and body hostage, I failed to suppress a snicker, causing Blake's smile to widen for a moment before his eyes grew solemn again.

"Eve is right, Silke's partly to blame for what happened, only it took me a while to see that. She should have kicked my big butt to weight-loss ther-apy but instead, she just kicked me out. She was never good at confrontation." His eyes, which had drifted off into the distance, refocused on mine and the smile that suited him so well crept back into his face. "Unlike you."

Despite his heartfelt smile, his words failed to as-suage my tormenting thoughts. Were my butt-kicking abilities all he appreciated about me?

"You just said I was nothing like Silke, and it's true in more ways than one," I began, my eyes struggling to remain on his. "See, my fear of ruining your diet wasn't all that held me back from telling you how I felt. I… I overheard you and Lars talking in the garage and thought you didn't feel what I felt for you. This is why I tried to make you leave as long as I was still capable of letting you go."

Again, Blake's fingers journeyed through his hair, leaving behind a nest-like arrangement. "This can't be happening."

Is that a good or a bad 'can't be happening'? Before panic had a chance to surface, however, I felt a pair of warm, strong hands tug at mine until I was straddling their owner as best as I could manage and breathing in the scent I had feared I would forever have to live without. In the same fashion, my body welcomed his one back, snuggling as deeply into his softness as possible.

"Ela, do you honestly believe I don't want you because you're skinny?" I heard Blake's voice over my shoulder eventually, causing me to pull back. His eyes were practically dancing with laughter. "Aside from being the smartest, bravest, strongest and most resourceful girl I've ever met, you're so beautiful that sometimes I can't believe you're for real." His warm hands grasped my shoulders. "*And* you're an FFA! I mean, how lucky can a fat guy get?"

"So, you're OK with it?"

"'OK with it'? I weigh around 500 pounds and you're into every single one – how can I not be OK with it?"

"Because... knowing how I feel might sabotage your diet."

His round face was alight with such joy and hope, it was heartbreaking. "Ela, listen: I'd never let myself go back to my old ways because I know I can't stay at this size if I want to live a long, healthy life. Still, can't you imagine how much pressure you've just taken off me? You know how frustrated I've been because I couldn't drop the pounds as fast as I wanted. I thought I stood no chance with you unless I made some visible progress. And now it turns out it's OK for me to take it slow and healthy because you find me hot already!"

"Mhm, extremely hot."

My hands immediately dove in to cosign the message and his body responded instantly. Within a few seconds, I felt the evidence of my arousal seep through my underwear and possibly through my jeans as well.

"We need to leave," I managed to gasp at some point.

"Yeah, we do."

Lars and Eve emerged from the kitchen when we left the living room in a state of unkemptness and dishevelment that would have done the homeless proud.

"We need to— "

Lars only grinned and waved the remainder of Blake's words away. "Be safe, kids."

He pulled Blake into a hug and, before I could react, me next. "Oh, shit, Ela, I'm sorry."

"No, it's..." I gulped, "it's… fine, I guess." I could touch him now, too? Next, I hugged Evelyn and then we were out the door. I would have ruminated on what had just transpired had I not had very different things on my mind now.

Somehow, I conveyed us home on one piece, treading the fine line between obeying life-preserving traffic regulations and the vociferous demands of my nether regions. Once at the house, it didn't take us more than a few minutes before we lay next to each other in a sweaty bundle, and no more than thirty seconds before my hands began wandering and kneading whatever they could reach.

"So, you find all that attractive, huh?" I heard Blake's lazy chuckle.

"Mm-hm."

My teeth pitched in for emphasis, causing him to wince before he pulled me close for another protracted kiss. For a while, nothing was to be heard other than our deep breathing.

"While we're in the confessional: I found your YouTube channel."

Instantly I lifted my head. "When?"

"Before we found out you could touch me," he smiled a mischievous smile down at me.

"And let me guess, you have watched all videos, including the one about exploring your tastes?"

"Yeah."

"Considering the outcome," I told him after a moment, "I can't really be mad at you. I'm just surprised you managed to keep it a secret. Usually, you're as readable as a book."

"I know. By the way, how come you can hug Lars and Evelyn now?"

"I have no idea, and for some reason, I've been… well, too busy to invest much thought into the matter."

"Can't blame you." He kissed the tip of my nose. "But what do you think now? What brought this on?"

"I don't know. I found out at the café where I was meeting with Eve before we came over."

"What were you doing the moment before you touched her?"

"Just talking."

"What about?"

"How much you're my type."

"Not that I wouldn't want to take credit for lifting the curse," he grinned, "but I don't get it. What's the pattern here?"

"Beats me."

I surrendered myself to the comfort of his doughy chest again, momentarily too content to explore the matter further. Blake was back and all was in the open now. Literally, I grinned to myself as I looked across the tangle of limbs.

"Ela?" The hesitant quality in his voice caused me to lift my head again. Naturally, his face mirrored his voice. "What happens now?"

Good question. Now that I could touch three people, my earlier tentative life plans had taken on a more definite shape.

"First," I began on a deep exhale, "I would like to see what it'll be like to *really* live together. Get a sturdy bed and move into the bedroom, for instance. Invite friends over. If that works out and if you agree..." I paused, momentarily insecure how my plans would be received, "I'd like to look for a condo or house for us in the city." The tightening of his arm around me encouraged me to go on. "I'm sure you'll be able to go to work again soon, and I've decided I'd like to become a diet coach for teenagers."

"You'll be terrific." Blake's lips pressed against the crown of my head. "Just stay away from their tubby fathers, OK?"

"OK," I smiled back before I grew serious again. There was one more thing I had planned and it came before everything else I had named. "But before we even look at a new bed, there is something else: I'd like you to meet my mother."

Chapter Eighteen
BBB

I nstantly Silke shrank away from the large window pane of the Aldi grocery store. Even though she had suspected her ex-boyfriend was still living in the area, he was the last person she had expected to see at this location. No, actually, he was the second-to-last person. The last one was the tall, dark-haired beauty with her slender arm around her companion's still massive but slightly diminished torso. Blake had found a new girlfriend, not even two months after their breakup.

The loving smile Blake sent the woman's way cut into Silke like a wicked blade and invariably her deeply buried insecurities reared their sneering heads again. Had she let go of a good man just because she had been too chicken to confront him about his eating when there was still a chance of a turnaround? What if she never found a man as loyal, gentle and funny as Blake who appreciated her the way she was?

The mismatched couple in the store, however, remained oblivious to Silke's gloomy reflections as they steered their shopping cart through the aisles, not an easy feat with half their limbs intertwined with each other. Aside from the dejected woman

255

outside, they were also drawing a great number of eyes, index fingers and comments from their fellow customers.

"People are probably wondering if I'll share any of this food with you," Blake murmured to his companion with a grin and a nudge of his wide hips against her narrow ones.

Ela, however, failed to muster an equal measure of equanimity. Even though she knew that the whispers in varying degrees of volume didn't hurt her boyfriend anymore, that didn't mean she would tolerate them. Experience had taught her cruelly that many other people did not possess such thick skin, and the gossipers needed to be taught a lesson before they truly injured their next victim. Perhaps running a stray finger over some of them would do the trick – finally an opportunity to put her condition to good use, she mused with a grim smile. Although tension still crept over her with tiny claws every time she remembered the upcoming visit to her mother, she had adopted an increasingly optimistic and constructive attitude towards her peculiar ability.

Nevertheless, each new unveiled comment or stare fueled Ela's corpuscles until the pulsing of her blood through veins and vessels thundered in her skull. Just a second before detonation, she abruptly disengaged her arm from Blake's and availed herself of a stray stool under a freshly hung price-sign holder.

"Alright, listen up, everyone!"

Instantly, a hush rippled through the small store like a rock thrown into a pond. The author of said silence now gestured between herself and her companion, whose round face had already begun to redden.

"Yes, we're together, and no, there is no money involved! I'm with this man because he is amazing, amongst other things in bed. Ladies, if you haven't been with a big guy, you've been missing out. And now continue shopping and leave us to do the same, OK?"

Ela's audience remained stunned into inertia, except for a few heads that ducked and a couple of cheeks that mimicked Blake's. The sound of sudden clapping and cheering abruptly transferred the quiet mass's attention to two heavyset women in their twenties as well as a rotund elderly gentleman before the discomfited crowd began to disperse. Blake turned to Ela, who had meanwhile descended, staring at her as if she were wearing a halo.

"On the one hand I'm afraid I can never show my face here again; on the other hand I've never been prouder of anyone." His lips met hers in a passionate kiss. "I love you."

"And I love you."

A smile that a narrow, skinny face would have struggled to accommodate spread across his fleshy cheeks as he pulled his girlfriend as close as his expansive midriff permitted. "I hope the ladies won't show up in hoards now, insisting on testing your theory."

Ela's eyebrows rose to an impressive height. "About a big guy showing them the time of their lives in bed? I hope they know I was speaking in the abstract. You are mine, and I can think of more than one way of making sure they understand that."

Their lips met again, their shared intimacy tender rather than tempestuous this time before they gently pulled apart again and resumed their leisurely stroll through the store and through the parting sea of intimidated shoppers. There were standing in line at the checkout when Ela felt a tap on her shoulder. It was the brunette, one of the two big women who had applauded her speech earlier. Her artfully made-up oval face was stretched into a smileful reminiscent of a groupie finally facing her life-long idol.

"I… I just wanted to tell you that your speech was the bravest and most romantic thing I've ever heard."

"Uh-huh, thank you," Ela answered, touched but also warily eyeing the way the woman's hands were fidgeting as if they longed to pull her into a hug.

"No, thank you," the brunette gushed, "you've made my day."

And before Ela could react, her fan's body made good on its promise and burst forth into a hug, her warm hands grazing the exposed skin on Ela's neck. Impulsively, Ela jerked and raised her hands like a shield.

"Sorry, I didn't mean to startle you."

"It's… it's OK."

Offering another bashful but nonetheless admiring smile, she walked off and rejoined her timid friend who had remained in the background.

"Did you see that?" Ela whispered to an open-mouthed Blake, paying no heed to their fellow shoppers' similar reactions.

"Yeah. Did she touch you?" he murmured back.

"She did, and nothing happened. Why the heck not?"

"Damned if I know."

And they never would know. Neither that it had been Ela's self-admission about her physical preferences that had lifted her condition for Blake, nor that confiding in Evelyn and Lars had done the same to them, nor that her public announcement had restored her to the world.

Naturally not every tormentor of big people required such drastic measures as had been applied to Ela, nor did they undergo such a profound change akin to a Saul-to-Paul-like conversion. However, Karma was proud of being able to produce an appropriate technique for each upon whom she zeroed in to – sometimes quite literally – even out the scales. Ela had been wrong: Karma is a bitch. A big, beautiful bitch.

Author's Bio

Sir Patrick is an investment banker and fund manager, in addition to that, he is a senior banking redemption officer and Judge who lives and writes from the United Kingdom. He is the author of several books in finance and Karmic Love is his debut novel.

Sir Patrick writes for the liberation of all people, focusing on the beautiful people who are often left out the literary world of creative writing.

Thank you again for purchasing this book, I hope you have enjoyed it!

Author: Sir Patrick Bijou